All of a sudden, the girls heard a loud gasp coming from the kitchen.

"What was that?" Mary asked.

Nancy looked at Bess and George. "It was Hannah! Let's go see what's happening! Come on!"

Hannah Gruen was the Drews' housekeeper. She had been with the family ever since Nancy's mother had died five years before. Nancy was positive that Hannah was the best cook in River Heights. She was also sure that Hannah gave the best hugs.

When the girls got to the kitchen, Hannah was just getting off the phone.

"Are you all right?" Nancy asked.

Hannah turned and looked at them. "I just got off the phone with Mr. Madison," she said sadly. "It looks like Thanksgiving won't be the same this year!"

Join the CLUE CREW
& solve these other cases!

Nancy Drew

and the Clue Crew®

#16

Thanksgiving Thief

By Carolyn Keene

Illustrated by Macky Pamintuan

Aladdin

New York London Toronto Sydney New Delhi

❦ ALADDIN

An imprint of Simon & Schuster Children's Publishing Division

1230 Avenue of the Americas, New York, NY 10020

First Aladdin Paperbacks edition September 2008

This Aladdin edition July 2015

Text copyright © 2008 by Simon & Schuster, Inc.

Illustrations copyright © 2008 Macky Pamintuan

All rights reserved, including the right of reproduction in whole or in part in any form.

ALADDIN is a trademark of Simon & Schuster, Inc., and related logo is a registered trademark of Simon & Schuster, Inc.

NANCY DREW and related logos are registered trademarks of Simon & Schuster, Inc.

NANCY DREW AND THE CLUE CREW is a registered trademark of Simon & Schuster, Inc.

For information about special discounts for bulk purchases, please contact Simon & Schuster Special Sales at 1-866-506-1949 or business@simonandschuster.com.

The Simon & Schuster Speakers Bureau can bring authors to your live event. For more information or to book an event contact the Simon & Schuster Speakers Bureau at 1-866-248-3049 or visit our website at www.simonspeakers.com.

Designed by Lisa Vega

The text of this book was set in ITC Stone Informal.

Manufactured in the United States of America 0615 OFF

10 9 8 7 6 5 4 3 2 1

Library of Congress Control Number 2007943606

ISBN 978-1-4169-6777-4 (*Thanksgiving Thief* pbk)

ISBN 978-1-4424-5920-5 (*Thanksgiving Thief* eBook)

ISBN 978-1-4814-6080-4 (*Mall Madness* and *Thanksgiving Thief* proprietary flip-book)

CONTENTS

Thanksgiving Thief

Chapter One

Cool Costumes

"Those poor turkeys!" eight-year-old Nancy Drew said. She was watching a story on the small television set in her room. "Someone needs to help them."

"What are you talking about?" asked Bess Marvin.

Nancy explained that some wild turkeys had been spotted in the parking lot of River Heights Elementary School late yesterday afternoon. When one of the school janitors tried to catch them, though, they ran away. No one was exactly sure where they had come from.

"I wonder why they were at our school," George Fayne said.

"The news showed them trying to drink some of the dirty water coming from a broken pipe," Nancy said. "I guess they were thirsty."

"Oh, poor things," Mary White Cloud said. "They need *clean* water to drink."

Nancy nodded. "It stinks that that broken pipe flooded some of the school offices, but I'm glad they canceled school today."

"Yeah! A three-day weekend!" exclaimed Bess. "We need the time to get ready for the pageant."

"Speaking of the pageant," George said, "we're all going to *be* turkeys if we don't pay more attention to what we're doing here."

Nancy giggled.

Bess twirled around in front of Nancy's mirror and looked at the beaded leather dress she was wearing. "I love being a Native American princess," she said. "This is so cool."

Mary White Cloud looked at Bess. "You look great!" she said.

Mary was a new girl in their class at school. She was Native American. The girls' teacher, Mrs.

Ramirez, had asked Mary to cast three more girls in the class to play Native American princesses in the pageant part of the River Heights Thanksgiving Celebration. Mary had chosen Nancy and Nancy's two best friends, Bess and George. Most of the time, everyone in River Heights knew the three of them as the Clue Crew. They solved mysteries in town that baffled everyone else. George and Bess were also cousins, although they weren't at all alike.

"The three of you are just right for the part. I hope this pageant is the best one ever at our school."

"We do too, Mary," Bess said. "Thanks for choosing us."

Nancy was always excited about the River Heights Thanksgiving Celebration. It was held at their school on the Wednesday before Thanksgiving. It gave the whole town a chance to celebrate the holiday together with a pageant, a feast, and a food fair.

"Now for the headbands," said Mary. She

opened a box on Nancy's bed and took out four beaded strips of leather. "These were worn by real Native American princesses in a tribal ceremony in Oklahoma last year," she told the other girls. "My uncle in Lawton sent them to me."

"Cool!" Nancy said. "Maybe they'll magically turn us into *real* princesses."

The four of them put on the headbands.

"Mine's a little tight," said Bess.

"That's because you have a big head," George joked.

"No, I don't," Bess retorted. "It's normal."

"Mine's a little loose," Nancy said. "Let's switch."

Finally everyone had headbands that fit perfectly.

"Where are the feathers?" asked Nancy. "Don't we have to have feathers?"

Mary nodded. "That's the most important part, but it's also the most difficult."

"What's so hard about finding feathers?" said George. "My pillow is full of them."

"It can't be that kind of feather," Mary said. "It has to be a special feather."

"What makes a feather special?" asked Nancy.

"It has to come from a *living* bird," Mary explained.

"You mean we're going to have to pull a feather from a real, live bird?" Bess exclaimed. "How are we going to do that? I don't think we should go around chasing birds, trying to steal their feathers."

"That wouldn't work, either," said Mary, "even if you could catch one. No, it has to be one that the bird left behind, just so it can be used in a ceremony."

"Birds do that?" Nancy said.

"That's what one of our legends says," Mary told them. "A bird will drop a feather somewhere, making a connection with the earth, and then we'll pick it up and put it in our headbands and use it when we're celebrating something important."

"Oh, I love that story," said Nancy.

"So do we," Bess and George chimed in.

"No one else in the pageant will be doing anything like this," Bess said. "All the Pilgrims are making their hats and bonnets out of black construction paper! How boring!"

All of a sudden, the girls heard a loud gasp coming from the kitchen.

"What was that?" Mary asked.

Nancy looked at Bess and George. "It was Hannah! Let's go see what's happening. Come on!"

Hannah Gruen was the Drews' housekeeper. She had been with the family ever since Nancy's mother had died five years before. Nancy was positive that Hannah was the best cook in River Heights. She was also sure that Hannah gave the best hugs.

When the girls got to the kitchen, Hannah was just getting off the phone.

"Are you all right?" Nancy asked.

Hannah turned and looked at them. "I just got off the phone with Mr. Madison," she said sadly. "It looks like Thanksgiving won't be the same this year!"

CHAPTER TWO

Pumpkin Problems

"Oh no!" Bess cried. "It's my favorite holiday!"

"Mine too," said Nancy. "Hannah cooks a great meal, especially the pumpkin pie."

"Forget my pumpkin pie this year," Hannah said. "There won't be any."

The girls looked at one another.

"Why not?" Mary asked.

"Somebody destroyed all of Mr. Madison's jars of pumpkin puree," Hannah explained. She shook her head. "Who would do such a horrible thing?"

Mr. Madison was the father of Katherine Madison, who went to school with the girls. Mr. Madison was also one of the chefs helping to prepare the Thanksgiving feast. It always took place in the school gymnasium, right after the pageant and before the food fair.

"Well, I'm sorry to hear that we won't have pumpkin pies at the feast, Hannah, but what does that have to do with *your* pumpkin pie?" Nancy asked. "Won't there still be cans of pumpkin puree at the market?"

Hannah stared at her. "Nancy Drew, are you telling me that you believed all these years that I was making my pumpkin pies from *canned* pumpkin?"

"Yes," Nancy replied, blushing.

"That's what my mother does," said George. "I thought everybody did."

Hannah shook her head in disbelief. "I only use Mr. Madison's fresh pumpkin puree. That's why my pies have won so many awards," she said. "Mr. Madison uses the puree when he bakes his pies for the feast, and then he sells the remaining jars at the food fair afterward."

"Well, this is terrible, then," Nancy said, "because your pies are the best!"

"We may not be smelling pumpkin pies this year," Bess declared, "but I'm smelling a mystery."

"That's for sure," Nancy said. "Let's get our bikes and head over to the school so we can talk to Mr. Madison."

"Would you like to come with us, Mary?" Bess asked. "The Clue Crew always welcomes other detectives."

Mary looked at the clock on the kitchen wall. "I can't," she said. "I promised Mom I'd clean up my room."

Hannah turned to Nancy. "That's not a bad idea," she said.

"I promise I'll do it as soon as I'm back, Hannah," Nancy said hurriedly. "When a mystery calls, the Clue Crew has to drop everything."

"Well, I'll agree with the *dropping* part," said Hannah. "It looks like that's what you did with all your clothes on the way to your closet."

"Speaking of clothes, we'd better change first,"

George suggested. "People will think the Clue Crew has become the Native American Princess Clue Crew."

"That's for sure," said Bess.

Nancy, Bess, and George said good-bye to Mary, then rushed to Nancy's room to change out of their costumes.

Within minutes, they were biking down the sidewalk toward River Heights Elementary School. The school was only four blocks from Nancy's house, so the girls were allowed to travel there alone, as long as they stayed together.

When they arrived, they left their bikes in the bike rack, locked them up, and headed for the gymnasium. All the doors were open because people were coming and going as they decorated for the upcoming festivities. The large kitchen was off to the left, between the gym and the cafeteria. That was where Nancy knew they'd find Mr. Madison.

"I see Katherine and her father," Bess said. "Katherine!" she shouted. "The Clue Crew is here to help!"

Katherine looked up and waved.

When the girls got closer, Nancy said, "We're sorry about what happened. Hannah is really upset too."

"She's not the only one," said Katherine. "Everyone Dad called felt the same way."

Mr. Madison nodded. "I think half the people in River Heights make their pumpkin pies from my puree."

"Who would do something like this?" Nancy asked.

"We think we know," Katherine said.

Nancy, Bess, and George looked at one another.

"You do?" said Nancy.

"Yes. Peter Patino," Katherine answered.

"Oh no!" George said. "He's one of the nicest boys in our class."

"This is terrible," said Bess.

"What makes you think Peter is guilty?" Nancy asked.

"My dad had to fire Peter's uncle James because he kept missing work at the pumpkin farm," Katherine said. "Peter was really upset about it," she added.

"Still, I just can't believe Peter would commit such a crime," Bess said.

"The Clue Crew doesn't convict suspects until we have the evidence," Nancy reminded her. She looked at Mr. Madison. "Do you mind if we look around?" she asked.

"Be my guest," Mr. Madison said.

As Nancy, Bess, and George walked around

the kitchen, Nancy said, "We need to make sure we don't destroy any evidence, so watch where you step."

"What are we looking for?" asked George.

"Footprints in the puree—probably *sneakers*, if Peter did do it," Nancy replied.

For the next several minutes they walked all around the kitchen, searching every inch of the floor in Mr. Madison's assigned area.

Finally, Nancy said, "Well, whoever did this must have stepped where he or she wouldn't leave any prints."

"Hey, look at this!" exclaimed Bess. She pointed to several blobs of pumpkin puree on the floor. "It looks like someone tried to make a finger painting. See these strange scratches?"

"It was probably just some little kid whose

mother or father was down here helping to cook or decorate," Nancy said. "I don't think it's a clue."

"What do we do now?" George wondered.

"We go talk to—," Nancy started to say.

"I found one!" Bess suddenly shouted.

Nancy and George stopped. Bess was standing at a side entrance that led to an alley.

"You found a footprint?" asked Nancy.

"No, I found a brown-and-gray *feather*!" Bess exclaimed. "Now I have one for my headband."

Nancy and George rolled their eyes at each other.

"We're in the middle of an investigation, Bess," George said. "You need to keep your mind on that."

"Come on, let's go find Peter Patino," said Nancy. "We have some questions to ask him."

CHAPTER THREE

Stolen Stuffing

Nancy and the Clue Crew left the school and headed over to Peter Patino's house, which was a couple of blocks away.

"That wind's chilly!" Nancy said. "I knew I should have worn my jacket."

George shivered. "It wasn't this cold when we left your house," she said. "Let's bike faster. We'll get there sooner, and it'll warm us up." Everyone knew that George could outrun—or outbike—anybody at River Heights Elementary School.

"Hey! Wait for me!" shouted Bess. "I'm not the athlete in this group."

When they got to Peter's house, though, Mrs.

Patino told the girls he wasn't there. "Since there was no school today, he said he was going to meet up with Ned Nickerson to talk about forming a bowling league, so he's probably at the bowling alley."

Ned Nickerson was in fourth grade at River Heights Elementary. He and Nancy were good friends.

"We'll bike over there, then," Nancy said.

"We have something important to ask him," Bess added.

"I wish you'd ask him something for me, too," said Mrs. Patino, smiling.

"What's that?" George asked.

"What time will he be home?" Mrs. Patino asked. "He left after breakfast, and he hasn't been back since."

Nancy looked at Bess and George. "That's interesting," she said.

The girls waved good-bye to Mrs. Patino.

"If we see Peter, we'll give him your message," Bess called to her.

When the Clue Crew was too far for Mrs. Patino to hear, Nancy said, "Peter is sounding more like a suspect all the time. If he's been gone since early this morning, he could have destroyed Mr. Madison's jars of pumpkin puree before he met up with Ned."

"We'll soon find out," said George.

When the girls got to the bowling alley, they parked their bikes in a rack, locked them up, and headed inside.

"There's Peter," Bess said, pointing to the last lane.

"Wow!" Nancy exclaimed. "It looks like half the boys in school are here too."

Peter looked up and waved when he saw the three of them walking toward him. "If you want to bowl," he yelled, "you'll have to start your own league."

When the girls reached him, Bess said, "We don't want to bowl, we want to talk to you about pumpkin puree."

"About *what*?" Peter asked.

Nancy looked around. "Could we talk in private?" she asked.

Peter wrinkled his brow. "Oh no, is the Clue Crew on a case now?" he said.

"As a matter of fact, we are, Patino," George told him. "We're investigating the destruction of Mr. Madison's jars of pumpkin puree in the school kitchen."

Peter blinked, then slowly narrowed his eyes. "Are you telling me that you think I did it?" he asked.

"Did you?" asked George.

"Why would I?" Peter said.

"Because Katherine Madison told us that you were upset about your uncle," George explained.

"Yeah, well, I was upset when Mr. Madison fired Uncle James, because it's hard for my uncle to get a job," Peter said, "but you know that I'd never destroy anyone else's property."

"Well, this is a criminal investigation, and that means we have to cover all bases," Bess said. "It's nothing personal, Peter."

Peter looked around. "I have to go," he said. "It's my turn to bowl."

"Wait, Peter! Can you prove you didn't do it?" Nancy asked. "Do you have an alibi?"

"Yeah, I can, and yes, I do," Peter replied. He turned and called, "Nickerson!"

Ned quickly hurried over to them. "Hi, Nancy! Hi, Bess, George. What are you guys doing here?"

"We're on a case," said Bess.

"And I'm a suspect," Peter said, "but I was just explaining to Nancy that you and I have been busy all day, recruiting guys for the bowling team."

"You think Peter committed a crime?" Ned said. "Come on, Nancy! Get real!"

"Well, we need Peter's alibi," Nancy replied.

"Sure thing. We started out really early this morning, looking for guys, and now we have a team that's going to burn the competition," Ned said.

"Good for you, Ned," said Nancy. She turned

to Bess and George. "I guess we'd better be going."

"Good luck with the investigation," Peter called to them as the girls headed out the door.

"Now what?" Bess asked.

Nancy looked at her watch. "Oh no! I forgot to ask Peter what time he'll be home, and I need to get home too," she said. "It's almost time for dinner, and I promised Hannah I'd clean my room!"

Nancy's father, Carson Drew, was a successful lawyer, so Nancy often discussed some of the

Clue Crew's cases with him. Over dinner, she told Mr. Drew and Hannah about their investigation.

"We thought Peter Patino was a suspect, but it turns out he has an alibi," Nancy said. She sighed. "We'd go back to the crime scene to look for other clues, but by now it's probably been compromised."

"What?" said Hannah.

Nancy grinned. "I heard it on television. That means people have probably walked all over the clues and destroyed them."

"Well, you've been in situations like this before, Nancy. You know that sooner or later evidence will turn up that'll help you solve the crime," Mr. Drew said. "Just keep on sleuthing!"

"The Clue Crew never gives up, Daddy!" Nancy assured him.

The next afternoon, Saturday, Nancy and the Clue Crew met Mary White Cloud at the gymnasium. Mrs. White Cloud was going to help them with their parts in the pageant when she finished making her Indian fry bread. While they were waiting, Nancy and the Clue Crew filled Mary in on what they'd found out about Mr. Madison's pumpkin puree.

"We didn't find any clues," Bess said, "but"—she pulled the feather out from behind her and showed it to Mary—"I did find this. It was left by some bird in the alley outside the school kitchen."

"That's wonderful! You're the first person to pick up a feather, Bess," Mary said. "That's special in our culture."

Bess beamed.

"I'm glad your mother wants to help us with our lines," said Nancy.

"Well, my mom has been in a lot of Native American pageants all across the country," Mary told them proudly.

"She knows how we should act."

Just then, they heard a commotion coming from the kitchen.

Nancy looked at everyone. "Come on!" she shouted. "Let's find out what's going on!"

When they got there, Mrs. White Cloud was talking to Mrs. Stanley, who owned a bakery in town.

"What happened?" asked Nancy.

"I just discovered that somebody got into the storeroom where I had put my special bags of turkey stuffing mix," Mrs. Stanley said. "They ruined every one of them!"

"Oh no, not again!" Nancy groaned. "Someone really is trying to destroy the River Heights Thanksgiving Celebration!"

CHAPTER FOUR

Disastrous Decision

"This is awful," Bess said.

"It most certainly is," Mrs. White Cloud agreed. "Everyone in River Heights has told me nothing tastes as good as Mrs. Stanley's special turkey stuffing mix, and I was really looking forward to eating it."

"Mom uses your special stuffing in our turkey every Thanksgiving," Bess told Mrs. Stanley. "She's going to be so upset."

George sniffed the air. "What's that smell?" she asked.

"Burned cake," Mrs. Stanley said. "Don't ask. It's a long story."

Nancy turned to Mary. "Could we practice

later?" she asked. "This mystery is getting more mysterious, and the Clue Crew needs to check it out."

Mary turned to her mother. "Is that all right?" she asked.

"It most certainly is," said Mrs. White Cloud. "I can teach the girls how to be Native American princesses any time, but the mystery of what happened to the stuffing mix can't wait." To Mary, she added, "The fry bread is done. We need to go on home now, but we'll come back later."

Mary and Mrs. White Cloud said their good-byes and left.

Just then, a huge black dog raced through the kitchen. He had white powder all over his nose. He made a couple of circles and then headed into the gym.

"Wasn't that Quincy Taylor's dog?" George said.

"I think so," said Nancy. "I wonder what he's doing down here."

"Quincy told me his dog has been jumping over their fence lately," Bess said. "He's afraid someone will dognap him if he doesn't stop that."

Nancy turned back to Mrs. Stanley. "Maybe we can solve the mystery of who destroyed your stuffing mix," she said. "We haven't solved Mr. Madison's crime yet, but we're still working on it."

"The two could be related," Bess pointed out.

Mrs. Stanley blinked in surprise. "What do you mean?" she asked.

"Mr. Madison's pumpkin puree was destroyed in this same kitchen yesterday," George reasoned. "We're investigating that case too."

"I hadn't heard about that. I was working in my bakery, trying to get caught up with holiday orders," Mrs. Stanley said. "That's just terrible! I use his pumpkin puree for my pumpkin pies."

"How did you discover that something had happened to your stuffing mix?" asked Nancy.

"Well, I came here to the school to do my part for the feast, but I also needed to bake a couple of holiday cakes for a customer," Mrs. Stanley explained, "so I put one in the oven, and then I started making the second one, but I was listening to my favorite station on the radio at the same time, not paying as much attention to what I was doing as I should, and I burned the first cake."

Bess sniffed the air again and nodded to George.

"So I opened the door to the alley, to let in some fresh air, and then I went back to work on the cakes," Mrs. Stanley continued. "When I finally finished with those, it was time to start adding the wet ingredients, such as turkey broth, to the dry stuffing mix for the feast, and that's when I discovered that someone had knocked over all the bags and scattered the stuffing mix all over the floor."

"Can you make some more?" Nancy asked.

Mrs. Stanley shook her head. "Unfortunately, no. I use specially aged bread crumbs and just the right seasoning. It takes a while. There's not enough time left between now and the feast."

"I think I know who's responsible for these crimes!" George shouted. "Quincy's dog!"

"Yeah!" Bess agreed. "He sure did look guilty when he raced through just now."

"Maybe he came through the door to the alley and got into the stuffing mix when you weren't paying attention, Mrs. Stanley," Nancy said. She turned to Bess and George. "I wonder if he's responsible for destroying Mr. Madison's pumpkin puree, too."

"We should find out if he has an alibi for that time," George said.

"We'll do that after we examine the crime scene," Nancy decided.

The Clue Crew started looking for clues.

After a few minutes George said, "I'm going to look out in the alley."

Nancy and Bess continued to search the storeroom and kitchen.

When George came back inside, she said, "Well, I know why Quincy's dog's nose was all white. There's a flour spill in the alley from where he was digging around in the trash can."

Nancy looked at the spilled bags of stuffing mix on the floor. "If Quincy's dog were the culprit, wouldn't there be signs of flour on some of

the bags in either the storeroom or the kitchen where he nosed them open?" she asked.

"You'd think," George said.

"Well, there aren't," Nancy told her friends.

"What if he came in here first?" asked Bess.

"I think someone would have noticed him earlier if he had come into the kitchen first," Nancy concluded. "I don't think Quincy's dog is our criminal."

"Another dead end." Bess sighed.

"Not for me," said George. She held up a feather. "I found one in the alley too, just like Bess did. Now I have a feather for the pageant!"

Later that evening, when Nancy and the Clue Crew went back to the gymnasium to practice their roles, the first thing George did was tell Mary about finding her brown-and-gray feather.

Mary let out a sigh. "You may not get to use it after all," she said.

"What do you mean?" Nancy asked.

"Well, Deirdre Shannon's parents are in charge of this year's celebration," Mary explained. "After they heard about the food being destroyed, they told Mrs. Ramirez that the entire event—the pageant, the feast, and the food fair—might have to be canceled. They're worried it's turning into a disaster."

CHAPTER FIVE

Cold Case

On Sunday afternoon, before Nancy left for the school to practice for the pageant, she told her father everything that had happened the day before.

"Do you think the two crimes could be a coincidence, Daddy?" Nancy asked.

"Well, there are such things as coincidences, Nancy, and the two might not be related after all," said Mr. Drew. "But don't give up on finding the culprits. Just follow the evidence and remember that things aren't always as they appear."

"Don't worry, Daddy," Nancy said. "The Clue Crew is still on the case! See you later." She grabbed her jacket and headed out the door.

When Nancy got to the school, some of the
other kids who had parts in the pageant were
gathered in little groups on the playground.
They were whispering to one another about the
possible cancellation.

"Don't worry," Nancy reassured the kids as she passed each group. "The Clue Crew is trying to solve the mystery."

Nancy finally found George and Bess by the swings. They were talking with Katherine Madison, Suzie Park, and Natalie Coleman.

"George and I found the perfect feathers, too," Bess was saying when Nancy joined them. "But if the celebration is canceled, we won't be able to use them in the pageant."

"Oh, that would be too bad," Natalie said.

"I love this time of the year," said Suzie, "mainly because of the celebration."

"Me too," Katherine said. "My dad and I were already upset about his pumpkin puree, and now if everything is canceled, we'll feel even worse."

"Try not to worry too much, girls," Nancy told them. "The Clue Crew hasn't given up!"

As Nancy, Bess, and George entered the school gym, Nancy said, "There's Mrs. Ramirez over by the stage. I need to talk to her. I'm going to run on ahead."

Mrs. Ramirez looked up when Nancy reached her. "Oh, hi, Nancy," she said sadly. "I suppose you've heard the news that the celebration may be canceled."

"It hasn't happened yet, Mrs. Ramirez," Nancy said, "and the Clue Crew is going to do everything possible to make sure that it doesn't."

"Thank you, Nancy!" said Mrs. Ramirez.

Just then, Deirdre Shannon walked up. "Oh, Nancy, isn't it just awful?" she said.

"Isn't *what* awful, Deirdre?" Nancy said.

"You haven't heard?" Deirdre exclaimed. "There may not be a River Heights Thanksgiving Celebration this year after all."

"Oh, *that*." Nancy smiled. "Well, the Clue Crew is on the case, Deirdre."

"That would be awesome if you solved it, because everyone is working so hard," she said. "I'm in charge of costumes for all the Pilgrim girls, and I'm trying my best to make them look stylish in those boring black dresses."

"Well, Deirdre, if anyone knows about fashion, it's you," said Nancy. "But I don't know if there's a lot you can do about what the Pilgrim women wore back then."

"You're probably right," Deirdre said. "I wish the Thanksgiving pageant was set in Paris or New York during Fashion Week."

"Don't count on that happening!" Nancy joked.

"Well, I have to go get my mom's fresh turkeys," Deirdre said. "Normally, she has to wait until the food fair, but Mr. Davidson, our butcher, said she could get hers today because she and Dad are so busy coordinating the celebration."

"Do you need any help?" Nancy asked.

"Sure," Deirdre said. "Those turkeys are heavy."

Nancy turned to Mrs. Ramirez. "Do we have time before the pageant practice starts?" she asked.

"Well, if the Clue Crew is going to save the celebration, then we'll have practice," Mrs. Ramirez said, "so we can certainly wait until

you've finished helping Deirdre with the turkeys."

Nancy and Deirdre headed toward the kitchen. When they got to Mr. Davidson's area, he wasn't anywhere to be found.

"I can't wait for him," Deirdre said. "I have so many things to do."

"Where does he keep the turkeys?" asked Nancy.

"They're fresh turkeys, not frozen," Deirdre explained, "so he just keeps them in his refrig-erator."

"Well, there's a big refrigerator over there," Nancy said. "The door's wide open."

They walked over and looked inside.

"Here are two big turkeys with my mom's name on them," Deirdre said. "I guess it's all right to take them."

Deirdre picked up one of the turkeys. "Yuck! It's all squishy, like it's still alive!"

"Let me see," Nancy said. Deirdre handed her the turkey. "You're right. It's not even cold."

Just then, a voice said, "What are you two doing?"

Nancy and Deirdre turned. Mr. Davidson was staring at them.

"I think someone left the door to your refrigerator open, Mr. Davidson," said Nancy.

Mr. Davidson rushed over. He took the turkey from Nancy. "Oh no!" he cried. He examined the other turkeys in the refrigerator. "They're all spoiled! Now all my butcher shop customers will have to eat *frozen* turkeys for Thanksgiving!"

"Oh, that's terrible!" Deirdre said. "I guess my parents really will have to cancel the—"

"Wait, Deirdre! Please don't say anything to them yet!" Nancy interrupted. "Just give the Clue Crew a little more time. We'll get back on the case right now!"

CHAPTER SIX

Clueless Clues

Just then, George and Bess came into the kitchen.

"We wondered what had happened to you," Bess said. "Mrs. Ramirez is ready for us to practice."

"Our plans have changed," Nancy told her friends. She quickly explained about the spoiled turkeys. "Somebody really is out to destroy Thanksgiving. This is no coincidence!"

"Why couldn't they attack some other holiday?" asked Bess. "Why did they have to choose my favorite one?"

"Thanksgiving is a holiday for people to give *thanks* for all they have," Nancy said. "That makes it doubly awful that someone is trying to wreck the celebration!"

"I agree," George said.

"Would you mind if we took a look around, Mr. Davidson?" Nancy asked. "The Clue Crew is investigating the other kitchen crimes."

"I wouldn't mind it at all, Nancy," Mr. Davidson replied. He was a big fan of the Clue Crew. "Nothing like this has ever happened before."

"Well, I need to go. . . . The pageant will go on!" said Deirdre.

"Tell your mother I'm sorry about the turkeys," Mr. Davidson said. "I'll make sure it doesn't happen next year."

When Deirdre was gone, Nancy said, "Do you know any reason why someone would do this, Mr. Davidson?"

Mr. Davidson shook his head. "No. In fact, I try to be nice to everybody. When Mr. Shannon said he was expecting a late delivery of cranberries and potatoes from a wholesale packer in Chicago, I told him I'd be glad to stay to make sure everything was put away. I left the back door open so the driver could bring the boxes inside, because I was busy preparing the fresh turkeys."

Bess looked at Nancy. "I wonder if we can connect the driver to the other crimes," she said.

"I know him. He's not a crook," said Mr. Davidson. "The way I see it, while he was busy bringing the boxes, someone slipped inside and hid until after I was gone and then committed the crime."

"Maybe the deliveryman left the refrigerator door open by mistake, and you didn't notice it," George suggested. "Maybe he was in a hurry and just didn't get it closed."

"No. He put the cranberries and potatoes in one of the storerooms," Mr. Davidson said. "He didn't need to open the refrigerator door. Anyway, I'm sure it was closed when I left early this morning."

Nancy walked over to the refrigerator and examined the handle. It didn't look very sturdy, and she was sure it wouldn't take much effort to open the door. The handle was also right next to the edge of a long table, which had several small white feathers and a *brown-and-gray* one beneath it.

"Is this where you plucked your turkeys, Mr. Davidson?" Nancy asked.

"It's one of the places," Mr. Davidson answered.

"What color were the feathers of your tur-keys?" she asked.

"They were all white," Mr. Davidson said. "Why?"

"I was just curious, that's all," Nancy said.

She couldn't believe it. The brown-and-gray feather was just like the ones Bess and George had found at the other crime scenes. She quickly put it into her pocket.

"Well, I guess we'd better be going," she said. "I think there's something we need to investigate." She turned to Bess and George. "Come on, let's go."

Once outside, Nancy took the feather out of her pocket and showed it to them.

"Wow!" Bess said. "Now all three of us have feathers!"

"That's not the point, Bess," Nancy said.

"It isn't?" said George.

"No," Nancy said. "Do you realize that we've found the same kind of feather at all three crime scenes?"

"Oh yeah!" Bess remembered.

"I think the thief is using feathers as his calling card," Nancy said. "He—or she—wants us to find them so we'll know it's the same person committing the crimes."

"Why?" George asked.

"Some criminals like to be known by things like that," Nancy explained. "When they read about 'the Feather Bandit' in the newspaper, they feel special."

"That's true!" Bess said. "You see it on television all the time!"

"Right!" George put in. She looked at Nancy. "What are we going to do about it?"

"We're going to tell Mrs. Ramirez that we need to do some sleuthing instead of practicing our parts, and then we're going to my house to do a little research on the Internet," Nancy said. "I want to find out if there have been crimes in other towns where feathers have been left."

ChAPTER SEVEN

Funny Feathers

The Internet didn't turn up anything on "feather bandits," so Nancy and the Clue Crew took their feathers to Mary White Cloud's house.

"This is the third time we've found a feather at the scene of a crime," Nancy told her. "We think it's the thief's calling card."

"Oh, I've heard about that on television," Mary said. She sighed. "I'm sorry, but if these feathers did come from a thief and we have the pageant, I don't think you can use them."

"Why not?" George asked.

"Well, if they were dropped by a thief instead of a bird," Mary explained, "then that means they're negative, not positive, and you always need to use positive feathers in a pageant when you're dealing with Native American culture."

"That makes sense," Nancy said. Bess and George nodded.

"We'll just have to start all over," said Bess. She looked at her feather. "It was so pretty, too."

"Do you know what kind of feathers these are, Mary?" Nancy asked.

Mary shook her head. "No, I don't. We don't always know what kind of a bird drops its feathers, but in our culture, it doesn't really matter, as long as the bird does it willingly." She looked at Nancy. "Is it important to your investigation?" she asked.

"I think it could be," Nancy said. She looked at Bess and George. "It might give us a clue as to who the thief is, if we knew where the feathers came from."

"What if the thief is just picking them up off the ground like we were doing?" asked Bess. "It might mean nothing."

"Or it might mean *something*," George said. "I

agree with Nancy. We should check this out."

"Well, you could ask Mrs. Fulton," Mary suggested. "She teaches science, so she might know about birds."

"That's a great idea," Nancy said. She looked at her watch. "We still have time. It won't be dark for another hour."

They used Mary's telephone to ask Mrs. Fulton if they could come over because they had something very important to talk to her about. She told them they could.

"See you later, Mary!" the girls shouted.

Nancy and the Clue Crew headed to Mrs. Fulton's house, which was down the street from Mary's.

When they arrived, Nancy rang the buzzer.

Mrs. Fulton opened the door. "Goodness, that was quick!" she exclaimed. "Come on in, girls."

The girls headed through the door.

"Well, to what do I owe the honor of your presence, Nancy Drew and the Clue Crew?" Mrs. Fulton said. "I don't think either my husband or I have committed a crime, although some of my students probably don't agree with me after that last test I gave them."

"We found some feathers," Nancy said. "We were hoping you could identify them for us."

"Well, I may be able to, if they're not too exotic," Mrs. Fulton said. "I studied ornithology in college, actually."

"Orni-*what*?" Bess asked.

"That's the study of birds, Bess," George said.

Nancy pulled the three brown-and-gray feathers out of her pocket and handed them to Mrs. Fulton. "Do you recognize them?" she asked.

Mrs. Fulton grinned. "Is this a Thanksgiving prank?" she said.

Nancy looked at Bess and George. "No, we're very serious," she said. "I'd rather not tell you where we found them, since it's part of an ongoing investigation, but we thought that you, as the expert, could help us with the case."

"Of course," Mrs. Fulton said. "They're wild turkey feathers."

"*Wild turkey* feathers?" the girls exclaimed.

"You're kidding," Nancy said.

Mrs. Fulton looked at the feathers again. "Nope, that's what they are," she confirmed.

"Well," Nancy said. She bit her lip in thought. "This is starting to make sense now. You've really helped—"

Just then, a man burst through the front door. "LOUISE! My green beans are ruined!"

Nancy and her friends looked at Mrs. Fulton.

"It's my husband," she said.

Nancy looked at Mr. Fulton. "Were your green beans at the elementary school, by any chance?" she asked.

Mr. Fulton nodded.

"Oh no," Bess said.

"Not again!" George added.

"What are you talking about?" Mrs. Fulton asked.

"We've seen this happen before," Nancy told her. She turned to Mr. Fulton. "Were your green beans supposed to be for the Thanksgiving feast?" she asked.

Mr. Fulton's mouth dropped open. "Yes, but how did you know?" he said.

"It's a long story," Nancy told him. "Can you tell us what happened?"

"My poor green beans! I work so hard in the summer, tending to them carefully, then canning them when they're ready, and then I put them in my garage until I take them to the school for the River Heights Thanksgiving Celebration," Mr. Fulton said. "People love my green beans!"

"Oh yes!" Bess said. "They're delicious, and I don't even like green beans."

"Let me guess. Somebody got into one of the storerooms and knocked all the jars off the shelves," said Nancy, "and now there won't be any, right?"

Mr. Fulton blinked. "Right," he said.

"Did you find any feathers at the scene of the crime?" Nancy asked.

"Yes, as a matter of fact, I did," Mr. Fulton said. "Wow! You girls really are great detectives!" He pulled some brown-and-gray feathers out of his pocket and handed them to Mrs. Fulton. "Do you recognize these?"

"Yes, they're wild turkey feathers," Mrs. Fulton said. She turned to Nancy and the Clue Crew. "Does this have anything to do with your investigation?" she asked.

"Yes, it does," Nancy told her. "We're looking for a person who wants to destroy the River Heights Thanksgiving Celebration and who leaves a wild turkey feather at the scene of each crime!"

CHAPTER EIGHT

Turkey Talk

The next morning, Monday, when Nancy's alarm went off, she sat up and stretched. The first thing she thought was, *We need to find out who in River Heights would have access to a lot of wild turkey feathers, and we'll solve the case.*

With that in mind, Nancy hopped out of bed, put on her robe and slippers, and, as she did every morning, opened her drapes to let in the sun.

Suddenly she gasped. Two wild turkeys were down on the front lawn, pecking at the dead grass, their bright red wattles flapping in the wind.

"Oh, wow!" Nancy exclaimed. "What are you two . . ."

Nancy didn't finish her sentence. All of a sudden, she was sure she was looking at the solution to the mystery the Clue Crew was investigating! But she also knew she had no real evidence—unless you could count the three wild turkey feathers—and how could she prove that they came from these two turkeys?

"I have to take you both into custody," Nancy whispered. "You may not like it, but if you two are out to destroy the River Heights Thanksgiving

Celebration, then the Clue Crew is going to stop you!"

Of course, what would happen once she had them in custody? Nancy wondered. How in the world would she ever figure out if they were missing any of their feathers? *Do feathers grow back?* Nancy thought. *Wow, these crimes get more and more complicated around here!* Still, it had to be done, Nancy knew. She slowly closed the drapes so she wouldn't spook the turkeys if they happened to glance at her upstairs window.

Next, Nancy hurriedly called both Bess and George and told them the same thing: "You're absolutely not going to believe this. You have to come to my house right away! And use the back door!"

Then Nancy returned to the window and peeked out again. For a minute she panicked because the two wild turkeys weren't where they had been, but she craned her neck and saw that they were over by a tree on the far side of the yard.

Suddenly the turkeys flapped their wings, as though they were trying to fly but couldn't. Then they headed for the street.

"Oh my gosh!" Nancy cried. "They're escaping!"

Nancy dressed quickly, then raced downstairs.

As she started for the front door, Hannah called, "Where are you going without your breakfast, Nancy Drew?"

"I'm on a case, Hannah! I don't have time for food!" Nancy said as she unlocked the door. At that moment, someone rang the back doorbell, and Nancy was sure it was Bess and George. "Please tell them to come this way, Hannah! I'm chasing two turkeys down the street!"

"You're *what*?" Hannah cried.

But Nancy was already running down the front porch steps. She could still see the turkeys. They were trotting down the middle of the street. A car coming toward them swerved to keep from hitting them.

"Nancy!" Bess called out from the front yard. "What's going on?"

"Hurry up!" Nancy shouted back. "I'll explain on the way!"

Just as Bess and George reached Nancy, the turkeys decided to change direction.

"They're headed for Suzie's front yard!" Nancy said.

"So what?" said Bess.

"So I think they're the ones who're trying to destroy Thanksgiving in River Heights!" Nancy replied.

"Turkeys?" said George.

"Yeah, *wild* turkeys," Nancy said.

Nancy and the Clue Crew reached Suzie's house just in time to see the turkeys fly over the side fence.

"I didn't know turkeys could fly," Bess said.

"They can't fly very far," George said.

"Yeah, just enough to create problems for us," said Nancy. "Come on!"

They ran toward the gate that led to Suzie's backyard.

"Maybe Suzie can help us," Bess said.

Nancy looked at her watch. "She's probably already at school. She likes to get there early to use the library."

George glanced down at her watch too. "That's where we should be, Nancy, *at school!*" she said. "Mrs. Ramirez said we were going to have a math quiz first thing."

Nancy had forgotten that. She needed a good grade on this one, too, because she had missed several problems on the previous quiz.

Now the girls were inside Suzie's backyard, and the turkeys were running around, looking for a way to escape.

"I think we have them," George said. "Here, turkey, turkey! Here, turkey, turkey!"

Suddenly the turkeys raced for the back fence, flapped their wings a couple of times, and were gone.

"Oh, great," Nancy said. "Well, let's see if we can find them on the next block!"

George pointed to her watch. "The time, Nancy, the time!" she said.

"We have to do this, guys!" Nancy told her friends. "We can't let them destroy Thanksgiving!"

Bess turned to George. "Nancy's right," she said. "We owe it to the citizens of River Heights, and that includes Mrs. Ramirez and her family!"

The Clue Crew raced out of Suzie's backyard, up to the corner, and over to the next street, where they saw the turkeys trotting down the center of the road.

"They're not going very fast," said Nancy. "They probably think they outsmarted us."

"They could also just be tired," George pointed out.

Just then, one of the turkeys turned its head and looked right at the girls. It made a loud gobbling sound to the other turkey, and the other turkey gobbled back. Then the two of them took off.

"What do you think they said?" Bess asked.

"The first one said, 'You're not going to believe

this, but they're behind us again!'" Nancy said, "and the second one said, 'You've got to be kidding me!'"

"I had no idea you understood turkey talk!" Bess giggled.

"Oh yeah," Nancy replied. "Come on."

For the next twenty minutes, the Clue Crew chased the turkeys all around the neighborhood, but then the birds seemed to vanish into thin air.

"Look at us," Bess said. "We're all sweaty and messy!"

Nancy glanced down at her clothes. "You're right. We need to go home and change."

"No, we don't," George said. "At least this way, Mrs. Ramirez might believe the story we're going to tell her."

As it turned out, Mrs. Ramirez did believe their story, but they still had to stay after school to take the test, and because they had missed part of school, their parents were also called.

"This is kind of embarrassing, Nancy," said Bess.

"Well, what's really embarrassing, Bess, is that we failed to catch the turkeys," Nancy said. She sighed. "If there's no Thanksgiving Celebration this year, then it'll be our fault."

ChaPTER NiNE

Sad Setting

When Nancy got home, Hannah said, "The school called. Your father will be upset that you got there so late." She shook her head. "I certainly hope you didn't look like that all day!"

Nancy told Hannah about chasing the wild turkeys all over their part of town. "I'm sure they're the ones responsible for what's been going on, but the only evidence we have so far are three feathers."

"Some evidence," said Hannah. She took a deep breath, let it out, then added, "Well, why don't you clean up before dinner?"

"Okay," Nancy said. She looked around. "Where's Dad?"

"He's working late at the office," Hannah told her.

"Oh, darn!" Nancy said. "I wanted to talk to him about the case."

"Well, it'll have to wait until morning," Hannah said, "because I have strict orders that you're not to stay up until he gets home."

Nancy was so tired, she didn't argue this time. Chasing two wild turkeys around River Heights was not something she did every day.

When Nancy awakened on Tuesday morning, she opened her drapes in hopes that the two turkeys had returned. But she saw only dead leaves being scattered by the wind.

Mr. Drew was already at the breakfast table, drinking his coffee and reading the newspaper, when Nancy went downstairs.

Nancy gave him a big hug, then sat down next to him and drank half the glass of orange juice Hannah had already put by her plate.

"I'm sorry about being late to school yesterday," Nancy apologized.

"It's not like you, Nancy, so I'm guessing you must have had a good reason. Hannah said you had something important to tell me about your current investigation," Mr. Drew said.

Nancy told him about the wild turkey chase. "But we finally lost them," she finished, "and we don't know where they went."

Mr. Drew thought for a minute. "So you think these two turkeys are responsible for all the destruction?" he said.

"Well, Daddy, it's really just a hunch, since the only evidence we have are three wild turkey feathers," Nancy told him. "But the fact that the turkeys were in town makes them suspicious."

"You're right about that, Nancy," Mr. Drew said. "I have an idea. I think I know where we might find these two birds—provided, of course, that they are responsible."

"Really?" Nancy said. "Can you take us there after school?"

Mr. Drew drained his coffee cup and replied, "Of course!"

That afternoon Bess and George went home with Nancy, where Hannah gave them an after-school snack. Then Mr. Drew drove them to the new city park, two blocks from River Heights Elementary School.

Nancy looked around, puzzled. "Why are we here, Daddy?"

"This is the only part left of what used to be a large area of wilderness. It used to stretch way out into the countryside," Mr. Drew explained.

"Really?" Nancy said.

Mr. Drew nodded. "This whole area was once all trees and bushes," he told the girls. He stopped the car. "Let's get out and look around. We'll need to be quiet, just in case our friends are around here, and I think they are."

"Friends?" asked Nancy.

"I don't consider anyone trying to destroy Thanksgiving a *friend,*" Bess added.

"Me either," George put in.

"Don't be so quick to judge," said Mr. Drew. "There are always two sides to every story."

For the next several minutes, the four of them made their way through the thick underbrush, trying to be as quiet as possible.

Suddenly Mr. Drew held a finger up to his lips, warning them not to make a sound. He slowly pulled apart a couple of branches and peered between them. "Nancy, look at this," he whispered.

"Oh my gosh!" Nancy whispered back. "I don't believe it."

Bess and George took turns looking. Then the four of them moved back, away from the thicket, so they could talk about what they had seen.

"They're the crooks, all right, Nancy," George said. "We've solved another case."

"Right," Nancy said. "We caught them red-handed with the evidence."

In the thicket, Nancy had seen the two adult wild turkeys, along with three offspring. They were surrounded by a bag of stuffing mix, some dried pumpkin puree, and piles of green beans.

"But that still doesn't explain who opened the refrigerator door and ruined all of Mr. Davidson's fresh turkeys," Bess said.

"Oh, I think it does, Bess," Nancy said. "If those turkeys are strong enough to carry some of that food here to the thicket, then I'm sure they'd be strong enough to fly up on that table where I found the feather and open the refrigerator handle with a foot or a beak."

"Wow!" George said. "I'm impressed with how smart they are!"

"Animals will do whatever it takes to survive," Nancy said. "Of course, they were probably shocked when they found other turkeys in the refrigerator!"

"Well, yeah!" Bess said.

Nancy turned to her father. "How did you know the turkeys would be here, Dad?" she asked.

"Well, like I told you, Nancy, this whole area used to be wilderness," Mr. Drew explained. "It was home to a lot of wildlife, including wild turkeys. Come over here," he said. "I want to show you something else."

They walked several yards to the edge of the park. They saw a group of new homes. "These housing additions were built where a lot of wild animals used to live," Mr. Drew said. "Now there's not enough land left to support them."

Nancy turned to Bess and George. "Well, the Clue Crew solved the mystery of who was trying to destroy Thanksgiving in River Heights," she said, "but now we have another problem. . . ."

CHAPTER TEN

Smart Solution

At school on Wednesday morning, the day of the festival, Mrs. Ramirez said, "Nancy Drew has an announcement to make."

Nancy came to the front of the room. "The people who were trying to destroy the River Heights Thanksgiving Celebration aren't people," she began. "They're *wild turkeys*."

The class gasped.

"Oh, I saw them on television!" Deirdre said. "They were drinking dirty water from that broken pipe here at our school."

"Right!" said Nancy.

She then told the class about the disappearing wilderness. She talked about how the Clue Crew had seen the wild turkeys in the last remaining thicket trying to feed their young.

"That's terrible," Katherine Madison said. "We can't let this happen to them."

"We need to do something about it," said Deirdre.

The rest of the class agreed.

"Well, here's my plan," Nancy said. "My dad says there is some land on the other side of the river. We're going to ask the City of River Heights to buy that land so the local wildlife, including turkeys, will have a place to live."

The class cheered.

"Why hasn't the wildlife already gone there?" Peter Patino asked.

"The river's probably too wide for some of them to swim across," George guessed. "But we honestly didn't ask them that question."

The class laughed.

"The wild turkeys will have a place to live and raise their families," Bess said. "And they won't have to come over to our school to steal food!"

"What will they do until we get the wildlife refuge ready?" Katherine asked.

"That brings me to the second part of my plan," Nancy continued. "We're going to feed them in the park every week until the wildlife refuge is ready. Who's with me?"

All the hands in the class went up.

While Nancy was making a list of volunteers, a couple of the other teachers came into the room. They huddled with Mrs. Ramirez, then left.

Mrs. Ramirez quieted down the class. "The other classes want to be involved too, Nancy, so we should have plenty of volunteers to make sure the turkeys are fed until they can be moved," she said.

Nancy grinned.

"Now, then, class, we're going to the gym to practice for the pageant," Mrs. Ramirez said. "I hope you haven't forgotten that the Thanksgiving Celebration is tonight."

"We haven't!" the class shouted.

That night Nancy, Bess, George, and Mary White Cloud were huddled in the wings behind the curtain.

George pulled the curtain back to peek out. "Oh, wow!" she said. "This place is packed."

"Let me look at you," said Mary. She adjusted their headbands. "Perfect. You really do look like Native American princesses."

"Do you have our turkey feathers?" Bess asked.

Mary nodded. "Your three and one Mr. Fulton gave me!" she said.

"Super!" Nancy said.

"I am now going to perform the feather ritual," Mary said. "I will put one feather at the back of each headband."

"Places, princesses," Mrs. Ramirez whispered. "You're on in two minutes."

Nancy Drew and the Clue Crew lined up behind Mary.

"I wonder if we would have found any feathers if those wild turkeys hadn't tried to destroy Thanksgiving," Bess whispered.

"I don't really believe now that they were trying to destroy Thanksgiving, Bess," Nancy whispered back. "I think they were just trying to get our attention."

"Well, they certainly did that," George said with a smile.

Then, on cue, the four Native American princesses walked out onto the stage, where they were welcomed by the Pilgrims.

Pumpkin Pie Pomander

A pomander is a mixture of great-smelling things packaged in a paper ball. A pumpkin pie pomander will make you think it's Thanksgiving all year when you hang it inside your closet or put it in a drawer.

You will need:

One orange

Two boxes of dried cloves

One tin or jar of pumpkin pie spice

Two sheets of tissue paper

Ten to twelve inches of orange or brown grosgrain (narrow) ribbon

One plastic food-storage bag

Two sheets of stickers with gold or silver stars and half moons, or two sheets with stickers that would appeal to one of your friends, if you plan to give the pomander as a gift!

❀ Before you start, you need to put on an apron, and then cover the kitchen table with newspaper. It's probably a good idea to secure the newspaper with tape. Then, when it's time to clean up, you can simply wad up the newspaper and throw it into the trash.

❀ First, stick the cloves into the orange, pushing them down as far as they'll go, until the entire surface is covered.

✳ Next, put the pumpkin pie spice in the food-storage bag. Add the clove-studded orange and shake gently until the orange is covered with the spice.

✳ Then wrap the orange in the tissue paper, tie it up with the orange or brown ribbon, and put it in a warm, dry place for about a month. When the orange is dried out, the pomander is ready to make your room smell like it's full of pumpkin pies!

✳ Now decorate the tissue paper with the stickers, and you're all set!

Mystery at the Mall?

Nancy pulled her purple notebook and matching purple pencil from her back pocket. She was glad she'd brought them along.

Opening the notebook to a blank page, Nancy wrote down *Missing Money Mystery*. Under that, she wrote two columns. One said *Clues* and a second said *Suspects*.

The girls then rushed over to Rodger.

"We want to help," said Nancy, holding her notebook firmly in her hand.

Join the CLUE CREW
& solve these other cases!

NANCY DREW
AND THE CLUE CREW®

#15

Mall Madness

BY CAROLYN KEENE

ILLUSTRATED BY MACKY PAMINTUAN

Aladdin
New York London Toronto Sydney New Delhi

❤️ ALADDIN

An imprint of Simon & Schuster Children's Publishing Division

1230 Avenue of the Americas, New York, NY 10020

First Aladdin Paperbacks edition July 2008

This Aladdin edition July 2015

Text copyright © 2008 by Simon & Schuster, Inc.

Illustrations copyright © 2008 by Macky Pamintuan

All rights reserved, including the right of reproduction in whole or in part in any form.

ALADDIN is a trademark of Simon & Schuster, Inc., and related logo is a registered trademark of Simon & Schuster, Inc.

NANCY DREW and related logos are registered trademarks of Simon & Schuster, Inc.

NANCY DREW AND THE CLUE CREW is a registered trademark of Simon & Schuster, Inc.

For information about special discounts for bulk purchases, please contact Simon & Schuster Special Sales at 1-866-506-1949 or business@simonandschuster.com.

The Simon & Schuster Speakers Bureau can bring authors to your live event. For more information or to book an event contact the Simon & Schuster Speakers Bureau at 1-866-248-3049 or visit our website at www.simonspeakers.com.

Designed by Lisa Vega

The text of this book was set in ITC Stone Informal.

Manufactured in the United States of America 0615 OFF

10 9 8 7 6 5 4 3 2 1

Library of Congress Control Number 2007934383

ISBN 978-1-4169-5900-7 (*Mall Madness* pbk)

ISBN 978-1-4424-5919-9 (*Mall Madness* eBook)

ISBN 978-1-4814-6080-4 (*Mall Madness* and *Thanksgiving Thief* proprietary flip-book)

CONTENTS

CHAPTER ONE

Back-to-School Shopping

"I just remembered that today's the day!" eight-year-old George Fayne burst out. "There isn't a second to lose." George was suddenly talking a mile a minute and pulling on her best friend Nancy Drew's sleeve. "We gotta go now!"

"But George," Nancy said in a normal voice that sounded almost snail-like compared to how fast George was talking, "I really want your opinion on these new sparkly red sneakers." Nancy had been in the middle of trying on a pair of shoes when George declared they needed to go. "Check these out," Nancy said.

"Love 'em," George replied, without even looking down. She let go her grip on Nancy's

1

sleeve. Nancy stumbled slightly backward, catching herself on a rack of rain boots while George rushed out of the shop. "Catch ya later," she called.

"Wait!" Bess Marvin jumped up from where she'd been trying on a pair of yellow and green strappy sandals. "You can't go off on your own!" she shouted after her cousin, waving her arms. "We promised Hannah we'd all stick together."

Hannah Gruen, Nancy Drew's housekeeper, had brought the girls to the mall for their back-to-school shopping. They each had a list and some money. The girls were supposed to buy the necessary items on their list and then meet Hannah at the food court for ice cream before going home. Even though the River Heights Mall was really safe for the girls to wander around by themselves, the rule was that they had to "stick together like glue."

They'd only begun to look around and already the glue wasn't sticking.

"I can't believe George just took off like that. You'd better forget about the shoes," Bess told Nancy. "We have to go find her."

"We'll catch up with her in a minute," Nancy said calmly as she slipped off the new shoes and handed them to the salesclerk.

While Nancy was waiting her turn at the counter, Bess hurried to the front of the store. She could barely make out George's short brown hair bobbing up and down as George worked her way through the crowd, heading farther into the mall.

"Don't worry, Bess," Nancy told her friend. Nancy finished paying for her new sneakers and carefully put the change back into her small purple wallet.

The second Nancy was done, Bess said, "Come on. We need to make tracks!" Bess pushed her blond hair out of her blue eyes. "There are so many people at the mall today, we might never find George again. We're gonna be in so much trouble."

"I know exactly where she went," said Nancy. She guided Bess down a corridor to the Pencil Box, a huge store that had all the latest back-to-school supplies on display.

There, standing in front of the window of the Pencil Box with her nose pressed against the glass, was George.

"I told you not to worry," Nancy said with a huge grin. She swung her new shoe bag around in front of her.

Bess breathed a big sigh of relief. "How did you . . . ? Oh, right! You're such a good detective. I should have known you would find her."

"I know your cousin pretty well," Nancy explained. "I figured that with all the back-to-school stuff in the mall right now, the Pencil Box would be showing all the brand-new computer models in their window." She smiled. "You know how gaga George is about computers."

"The mystery of where George hurried off to is solved!" Bess laughed.

"This wasn't a real mystery. When there is

a real mystery to solve, it takes all three of us to figure it out," Nancy replied. She tucked her hand into the back pocket of her jeans to make certain she'd remembered to bring along her purple clue-collecting notebook. It was stuffed in there, just like always.

"The Clue Crew rocks," Bess agreed. "So far, we've solved all our cases."

"I wonder if there will be a mystery for us today," said Nancy thoughtfully.

"I doubt it," George remarked, finally turning away from the computers to look at Bess and Nancy. "Sorry I ran off like that. I remembered that the Pencil Box was going to display the latest GT XP105 computer in its window. The new 105 has a Running Man processor and a half-hose driver!"

"A half hose?" Bess said with a giggle. "That doesn't sound good at all."

"Oh, but it's the best!" George gushed. "The half hose connects the—"

"Whoa!" Nancy interrupted with a grin. "It's

okay, George. You don't have to tell us all the details. We're just happy that you're jazzed about the half-hose thingy."

"But from now on," Bess declared, putting her arm around George, "we gotta stick together like glue. Okay?"

"Sure," George agreed. She slung one arm over Bess's shoulder and another around Nancy. "Just like superglue."

CHAPTER TWO

Great Gumballs

"As long as we're already at the Pencil Box, why don't we pick up our notebooks, paper, and pencils?" Nancy suggested.

"Nah," Bess told her. "Let's go over to Schneider's department store first to get our backpacks. Then, when we come back here, we can put our supplies straight into our new packs and it'll be easier to carry all of it. I saw an orange wheelie backpack that looked amazing in the store's catalog." Bess smiled as she thought about the backpack. "I'm planning to take off the smaller wheels that come with it and attach big, snazzy, in-line wheels instead."

"Always the inventor," said Nancy, winking at Bess.

"I can switch out your wheels too, if you want," Bess offered.

"That would be great," Nancy answered.

"Before we go to Schneider's," George said, pulling Bess and Nancy along as if they really were stuck together, "let's go to the back of the Pencil Box and buy some gum from the Drop Zone."

The Pencil Box's six-foot-high Drop Zone was an incredible gumball machine. Each piece cost just a quarter, but before the gum came shooting out the bottom, it had to drop through three different levels of spinning, twisting, and flying tricks. Everyone loved buying gum from the Drop Zone machine.

The girls agreed that they desperately needed some chewing gum and, still linked together, began to work their way toward the back of the Pencil Box.

"Hey, Rodger." Nancy broke out from under

George's arm to greet the teenage boy who lived next door to her. He was standing at a checkout counter, wearing a blue "Pencil Box" T-shirt.

"Hey, Nancy," Rodger Hunter echoed in a cheery voice. Nancy had always liked him.

"Whatcha doing?" Nancy asked.

Rodger explained that his dad was best friends with Mr. Gustavson, the owner of the Pencil Box. "I need to make some money, and Mr. Gustavson needed some help with the back-to-school sale. So he gave me a job here." Rodger sounded glad to be working at the Pencil Box.

Bess pressed toward the counter where Rodger was working. "Rodger, are you using a new cash register?"

Rodger looked down at the machine on the counter in front of him. "I guess it's new," he said with a shrug. "It's my first day here, so I don't know for sure."

Leaning in for a closer look at the register,

Bess said, "No. It's not new. It's the same old machine as last year, but it's been fixed up, and some extra buttons were added." Her eyes lit up like lightbulbs. Just like George loved computers, Bess loved inventing and reinventing things. She liked taking apart old things and making them better, or faster. And most of all, Bess loved fixing up old machines.

"How does it work?" Bess asked Rodger excitedly. "Can you show us what it does?"

Bess stretched over the counter as far as she could to get a better view while Rodger explained. "As you put money in the drawer, the cash register figures out exactly how many dollars, quarters, dimes, nickels, and pennies go in. It calculates the change you need and spits the coins into this little cup." He pointed to a plastic dish on the side of the machine. "You never have to count money or add or subtract or anything like that. The cash register does it all for you."

George leaned in next to Bess. "It sounds like

there must be a computer chip in that cash register!" she exclaimed.

"There is," Rodger agreed with a confident tone. "Even though it's my first day, Mr. Gustavson put me in charge of this register. He said that all the money in it is my responsibility."

"Wow," said Bess, her eyes sparkling. It was clear to everyone that she'd like to be responsible for such an amazing machine.

"Cool," George exclaimed.

She also wanted to be in charge of the newly computerized cash register.

Bess and George would have stayed there all day watching Rodger ring up sales if Nancy hadn't said, "We only have half an hour left before we need to meet Hannah. Come on, girls, let's get the gumballs and run down to Schneider's to pick up our backpacks." She pulled George and Bess away from Rodger and the cash register while waving good-bye to him.

They headed down Aisle Twelve, past the notebooks, folders, and pencils, toward the towering gumball machine.

The girls were not surprised to find a line in front of the Drop Zone. Ned Nickerson, a fourth-grade boy from their school, was up. He was watching his gumball pass the second level, across a spinning platform that flung the gum into a small hole, heading toward level three.

Another girl from school, Deirdre Shannon, was waiting for her turn to buy gum. She was holding a small, heart-shaped tin box. The lid

was open, and everyone could see that the box was full of quarters.

"I hope she's only buying one," Bess whispered to Nancy. "We don't have all day to wait for Deirdre to buy so many gumballs."

The girls got lucky, and Deirdre bought only one gumball with a quarter she pulled out of her pocket, not from the tin.

"How's your summer vacation going?" Nancy asked Deirdre as she passed by.

"Great! I'm so lucky. My mom has brought me here practically every day to get gum," Deirdre reported. She popped a light blue gumball into her mouth, adding, "I'm off to buy some sweaters for school. See ya."

After Deirdre left, it was Bess's turn. She dug around in her purse for some change. She was just about to drop in a quarter and start the gumball fun when Mr. Gustavson, the store owner, came out of the back office carrying a roll of receipt paper.

Mr. Gustavson was a nice man—a little round

like a marshmallow, but always dressed neat and clean. No matter how busy the store was, Mr. Gustavson took time to visit with his customers and was always very, very friendly.

But today something weird was going on. Mr. Gustavson's face was red. His breath was huffy. And he was stomping, not walking.

The girls watched him as he clomped across the store. He didn't even turn to say hello. And Mr. Gustavson *always* said hello.

When he disappeared down Aisle Twelve, Nancy turned to Bess and George, who were still staring after him. "You know," she said with a curious look, "I have a hunch that there really might be a mystery to solve today."

ChaPTER THREE

A Mighty Mystery

"We have a big problem," Mr. Gustavson said to Rodger. He was speaking so loudly, the girls couldn't help but overhear.

They were chewing on their Drop Zone gum and heading toward the front of the store when they first heard Mr. Gustavson's voice. Now, as they came out of Aisle Twelve, Nancy, George, and Bess could see the store owner standing in front of Rodger and the amazing cash register. His hands were on his hips. "We have a big, big problem," Mr. Gustavson repeated.

"What's the problem?" asked Rodger.

Mr. Gustavson waved the roll of paper he was carrying. "This is the problem," he said slowly.

"The new cash register added up everything you sold so far today and told me exactly how much money should be in the drawer. Then the machine sorted the money and reported how much money actually is in the drawer." Mr. Gustavson huffed. "This"—he showed Rodger the numbers on the paper he was carrying— "shows that eight dollars and seventy-five cents is missing."

"I don't understand," Rodger said, looking at the numbers with his eyebrows pulled tightly together.

"Neither do I," said Mr. Gustavson. "You've been here all day working the new cash register." He pointed at the machine. "Do you have any idea what could have happened to the money, Rodger?"

"I don't know," Rodger said, sounding worried. Then, as if a lightbulb had gone off in his head, he suggested, "We should ask Robin if she has an idea. She worked this register while I ate lunch."

"Robin has been working here for three years," said Mr. Gustavson. The girls knew that they were talking about Robin Miller, the stock girl. She was really friendly and always helped customers who couldn't find something.

"Robin is a great employee. Money has never disappeared while Robin was at the register,"

Mr. Gustavson told Rodger. "Maybe, when you weren't looking, someone took the money. Or maybe by accident you rang up a sale wrong," he suggested.

"I was really careful. I don't understand what happened." Rodger groaned.

"I don't think you took the money, Rodger, but when you came to work today, I told you that all the money that went in and out of this cash register was your responsibility," Mr. Gustavson said. "That means you will have to give me back eight dollars and seventy-five cents from the money you earn today."

Rodger looked upset.

"Unfortunately, I have to take the money out of your paycheck tonight," Mr. Gustavson told Rodger. Then, with one last huff, he turned and walked right past the girls, back down Aisle Twelve, and into his office near the Drop Zone gumball machine.

Nancy looked at Bess and George. They all were clearly thinking the same thing.

"Maybe the Clue Crew can help Rodger," Bess whispered to her friends.

"He looks so sad," George commented.

Nancy pulled her purple notebook and matching purple pencil from her back pocket. She was glad she'd brought them along.

Opening the notebook to a blank page, Nancy wrote down *Missing Money Mystery*. Under that, she wrote two columns. One said *Clues* and a second said *Suspects*.

The girls then rushed over to Rodger.

"We want to help," said Nancy, holding her notebook firmly in her hand.

Rodger looked at Nancy, Bess, and George with a sad face and downcast eyes. "How could you possibly help me?" he asked. But before Nancy could reply, Rodger saw the notebook in her hand. His eyes perked up, and his frown flipped over into a smile. "Nancy Drew and the Clue Crew!" he exclaimed. "I almost forgot you guys are detectives! Can you help me solve this mystery?"

Roger definitely wasn't sad anymore. He looked hopeful now. "Did you hear what happened? Did you hear what Mr. Gustavson said about the missing money?"

"Every word," George said.

"We didn't mean to listen to a private conversation," Bess told him.

"Mr. Gustavson was talking really loud," Nancy put in. "It was hard *not* to listen."

Rodger grinned. "Can the Clue Crew really figure out what happened to Mr. Gustavson's eight dollars?"

"And seventy-five cents," added Bess.

"We'll try our best to find the missing money for you," Nancy told Rodger. "Tell us about—" A beeping sound interrupted her.

It was Bess's watch. She'd built it herself from a kit George bought for her online. "Oh no!" Bess exclaimed. "It's time to meet Hannah for ice cream and we never did get over to Schneider's department store to look at the backpacks. Or actually buy anything on our lists."

"It's all right," said Nancy. "Hannah will understand about the lists. But she won't understand if we are late to meet her at the food court." She looked up at Rodger, who was a good foot and a half taller. "We gotta run, Rodger."

"When are you coming back?" Rodger asked.

"We'll meet you back here in an hour," George assured him.

"We will help you solve this missing money mystery," said Bess as she set her watch to beep in another hour.

"Don't worry, Rodger." Nancy reached up and patted Rodger on the shoulder. "The Clue Crew is on the case."

ChaPTER FOUR

Flavor Saver

While the girls ate ice cream, Nancy told Hannah all about Rodger's missing money mystery.

"Sounds like you girls have some work to do," Hannah commented.

"Yeah," Nancy said, wiping her face with her napkin. "Can we head back over to the Pencil Box after we finish our ice cream? We promised Rodger we would."

Hannah glanced at her watch. "I don't know . . . it's getting late. The only thing you girls have bought so far is a pair of shoes for Nancy. I promised Bess and George's mothers that we'd get their backpacks and school supplies today. Why don't you girls let the mys-

tery wait until tomorrow morning? We could come back and—"

Nancy gave Hannah a pleading look. "By tomorrow some of our clues might have disappeared."

"Plus, Mr. Gustavson is going to take the money away from Rodger today," George added.

"We've gotta check things out now," said Bess. Her voice sounded a little higher than usual. "It's important."

"Oh, all right, girls," Hannah agreed with a small sigh. "I can see that you won't get anything else done until you've gone and investigated. I'll call Bess and George's mothers and let them know that we're going to have to come back again tomorrow to finish—I mean to start—our back-to-school shopping."

"A perfect plan," Bess cheered as she stuffed the last bite of her ice cream cone into her mouth and then picked up the gum she'd gotten from the Drop Zone machine. She had

taken the chewed-up piece out and put it in an empty water cup while she enjoyed her double ripple fudge cone.

"Eww," she said as she moved the gum around in her mouth, chomping a few times. "This gum has no flavor!"

"Gross." George stuck out her tongue and made a face at her cousin. "Nancy and I threw away our gum. It's disgusting to save ABC gum."

"It seemed like a good idea at the time," Bess remarked, spitting her gum back into the cup and throwing the cup away. "But now I know better. The Drop Zone gum definitely doesn't hold its flavor."

The girls arranged a new meeting time and place with Hannah. When they were done with the mystery, they'd find her by the exit to the mall. Then they hurried back to the Pencil Box.

Rodger was still right where they'd left him: standing at the new cash register, ringing up sales, and looking completely bummed out.

His face perked up a bit when he saw Nancy, Bess, and George entering the store.

"Did you solve the mystery yet?" he asked in a rush.

Nancy replied, "We just got back. We need to look around for clues."

"Where should we begin?" Bess whispered to George and Nancy, glancing blankly around the crowded store.

Nancy took a minute to survey the scene. The Pencil Box was crowded with shoppers. There were a lot of kids from their school wandering the aisles with their moms or dads, pushing carts filled with stuff from the school supply list.

Nancy and the girls saw Nadine Nardo lugging her basket full of three-hole folders. Shelby Metcalf was checking out a fancy leather binder. Trina Vanderhoof was picking up some glue and colored paper. And Ned Nickerson was still there, chewing gum, looking at colorful book covers. He was holding up one with a skull and crossbones design on it.

"Should we interview Ned?" George asked. "He was here at the same time we were earlier. Maybe he saw something suspicious."

"Good idea." Bess patted George on the back. "Let's go." The cousins headed off until they realized Nancy wasn't with them.

Nancy was staring at Rodger and the cash register.

"Earth to Nancy." Bess waved a hand in front of Nancy's face.

"Come in, Nancy." George gave her a little push on the arm.

"Oh," said Nancy, giving her head a shake and coming back down to earth. "I spaced out for a second."

Bess laughed. "It's okay. We're used to it, since it happens every time we're on a case. You zone out and get all clumsy."

"I'm not clums—" Nancy began as she twisted quickly around to look at Bess.

Crash! Her left arm hit a display of masking tape and knocked the whole thing over to the

floor. More than a hundred rolls of tape spun out like little wheels, traveling at top speed across the slick white floor.

Nancy looked shocked for a second, then laughed. "Okay, so maybe I am a little clumsy and spacey when I'm thinking." Dropping

to her knees, Nancy began crawling around, collecting rolls of tape.

"Truth is," Bess said with a wink, "you're always thinking!"

George bent down and put her arm around Nancy's neck, saying, "Never change, Nancy Drew. We like you just the way you are." She smiled. "And we'll always be here to help clean up your messes." George pulled back her arm and began picking up rolls of tape too. "That's what friends are for!"

Robin Miller, the stock girl, saw the mess on the floor and came over to help Nancy and the girls. She set the display case back up and started putting in the rolls of tape that the girls collected. Her long, dangly earrings swung low beneath her spiky blond hair. There was an MP3 player hanging around Robin's neck, like a necklace, and earbuds in her ears. Robin was wearing a Pencil Box shirt and blowing gum bubbles as she worked.

Pop! Pop! Pop!

For every ten rolls she put into the display, Robin blew a new bubble. Ten bubbles later, everything was put back, the way it was before.

Bess and George thanked Robin for her help, and Nancy promised to be more careful.

Bess pulled Nancy into a big open area away from anything dangerous or breakable. "Now," she said when they were standing in a safe place, "what were you thinking about before you knocked over the tape display?"

Nancy was silent.

George tried to get her attention again. "Do you want to interview Ned?"

At that, Nancy came back to earth again. "Wait a minute," she replied, though she still had that spacey look in her eyes. "Oh yeah," she said after a long minute's pause. "I remember what I was thinking earlier. Before we do anything else, we have to check out that new cash register. I think it holds the secret to this mystery."

"In order to take a good look," said George,

"we're going to have to get permission from Mr. Gustavson."

"Let's go see him," Bess suggested. "Hopefully, he's not grumpy anymore."

The girls hurried toward Mr. Gustavson's office. On the way, they saw that Ned had finished picking out his book covers and was back in line for the Drop Zone.

"More gum?" Nancy asked Ned, before knocking on Mr. Gustavson's office door.

"Yeah," Ned replied. He shook his head. "This gum doesn't hold its flavor."

Bess sighed and agreed wholeheartedly. "I know," she told him. "It's all about the Drop Zone show and not really about the gum."

Ned smiled. It was his turn in the line. "Yeah," he said. "It's a great show. Totally worth a quarter."

The girls stayed a minute longer to watch Ned's gumball flip and twist and spin before falling into the bottom cup. Ned grabbed the gum and popped it into his mouth before say-

ing he had to go find his mom. He explained that they'd been at the mall all day.

"I had a ton of quarters this morning," he bragged. "I bet I bought ten pieces of gum today. Maybe even eleven! Every time my mom was in line at a store to buy something, I'd run over here to get another piece of gum." He pulled his pockets inside out. "Too bad I

used all the quarters I had in the gum machine. I should have saved some for the video arcade.

"Can you believe that my mom says we have to come back to the mall tomorrow?" Ned complained, like returning to the mall was the worst torture he could imagine. "I'm going to need more quarters. Drop Zone gum makes everything better. Even back-to-school shopping."

Nancy shook her head at him, then knocked on Mr. Gustavson's door.

"Come in!" he answered right away. The store owner was sitting at his desk, looking at a catalog.

Bess quickly explained that the Clue Crew was on the case of Rodger's missing money. George told him that they needed to examine the cash register.

"I think the answer to this mystery is inside that cash register," Nancy said.

"The machine has been totally fixed up," Mr. Gustavson told the girls. "It's perfect. There is no way that register made any mistakes."

"Even so," Nancy said. "We'd love to take a look."

Mr. Gustavson thought for a moment, then said, "Hmmm. It's very busy in the store right now. Today's really not a good time. Sorry, girls."

"How about tomorrow? We could come back before the store opens," Nancy asked quickly. Hannah had already agreed to bring them back to the mall to finish their back-to-school shopping. Surely she wouldn't mind bringing them early so that they could finish investigating this mystery.

Mr. Gustavson was silent for a few seconds, then said, "Well, I suppose that would be all right. I don't have to take the eight dollars and seventy-five cents from Rodger's paycheck today." He rubbed his plump belly. "It would be great if you girls could figure out where the money disappeared to."

"So we can come in the morning to investigate?" Bess confirmed.

Mr. Gustavson agreed to meet them at eight thirty. He was planning to come in early anyway to check on supplies. They could look around for a full hour and a half before the store officially opened.

"Great!" George cheered.

On their way out of the Pencil Box, Rodger waved at the girls. "So?" he asked. "Did you find any clues?"

"We haven't started looking around yet, Rodger," Nancy told him. "But Mr. Gustavson told us that he won't take the money from your paycheck today. He's giving us another day to investigate."

Nancy pulled out her notebook and looked at the page that said *Missing Money Mystery*, *Clues*, and *Suspects*. So far they had nothing to write down. The page was still blank, except for the headings.

"Tomorrow," she reassured Rodger. "The Clue Crew will definitely solve this case tomorrow."

ChaPTER FiVE

Clue Number One

"Where is he?" George complained as she paced back and forth in front of the Pencil Box's locked door.

Bess checked her wristwatch. "It's eight forty-one. He should be here by now."

Nancy looked up and down the mall, as far as she could see. Hannah was sitting on a comfy couch in the waiting area by the elevator. She'd brought some knitting to entertain herself while the girls worked on solving the money mystery. But other than the three of them and Hannah, they didn't see anyone else in the mall. Only a few employees had arrived and the doors had just been opened.

"Mr. Gustavson promised he'd be here to show us the register," Nancy remarked. "I'm sure he's just stuck in traffic or overslept or something like that."

"Maybe we should call his house," George suggested as she turned around to pace in the other direction for a while.

"I think we—" Bess began, but then stopped as a very out-of-breath Robin Miller came running through the mall, headed their way.

"My bad," Robin said by way of apology while she bent down to insert a key in a low lock on the shop's door. "Mr. Gustavson asked me to open the store for you this morning. He said he wasn't going to be here early like he thought and that I should let you look around. But when I was ready to leave home this morning, I couldn't find my keys." She pulled the keys out of the lock and jingled them near Nancy's nose. "You are not going to believe where they were! Last night, after work, I ran outta here to go meet some friends at the concert in River Heights

Park. You know, the free show they have every week before school starts?"

She stuck her keys into her pocket as she continued, "The concert was awesome, but I had skipped dinner and was starving when I got home. I guess that when I made myself a snack, I accidentally left my keys inside the fridge!"

"That's funny," Nancy said with a laugh. "We're just glad you're here. We're anxious to take a look at the cash register."

"You mean the new, amazing, computerized cash register?" Robin pushed open the door to let the girls inside. "Why'd ya want to look at that? It's empty now. Won't have money in it till right before opening time when Mr. G arrives." She stopped, but just long enough to breathe. "Mr. G didn't explain to me why you're here. He simply said I needed to let you in."

"Well," George began. "We're the Clue Crew, and we—"

"That's so cute!" Robin interrupted. "You guys belong to a club! Do you have a club T-shirt or jacket? I like to paint and could make a design for you." She pointed at her own Pencil Box T-shirt. "I drew the pencil and the box design for our work shirts," she said proudly. "And I picked the blue shirt material."

"It would be great to have our own shirts. Maybe we could make matching hats, too!" Bess exclaimed, totally into the idea. She loved fashion. "If you made us T-shirts, what color fabric would you use?"

Before Robin could respond, George gave Bess a little push and said, "We aren't design-ing shirts today."

"Oh yeah." Bess sounded disappointed, but then she saw the cash register sitting on the nearby counter and perked up.

"So, is this some kind of club project you guys are working on?" asked Robin.

Nancy was surprised that Mr. Gustavson hadn't told Robin why they were at the store so

early. She started to explain. "Actually, we're here to look for—"

"Are you preparing for Miss Kimler's big project?" Robin interrupted. "I had her for language arts when I was at River Heights Elementary."

"School hasn't even started," said Bess.

"We aren't working on a project," George added, but Robin wasn't listening. She pulled her MP3 player out of her pocket, hung the strap around her neck, and tucked the earbuds into her ears.

"It's going to be another busy day at the store," she said, shifting gears. "Back-to-school shoppers will be arriving soon, and I'd better get the shelves filled up with supplies." She pointed at the register. "Have yourselves a good look-see. Feel free to push the buttons. I'll reset the register when the store opens."

Then, before walking off, Robin gave Nancy a long, hard stare. "Be careful not to break anything." It was clear that she was thinking about the rolls of spilled tape from the day

before. And with that warning, Robin turned up the volume on her MP3 player, started to sing along to the tune, and disappeared down Aisle Twelve.

Bess walked around the counter to get a closer look at the cash register.

"Awesome," she muttered under her breath, as if she'd never seen anything so wonderful in her whole life. She pressed the on button along the side, and the front of the register began to glow.

"Holey moley," George nearly shouted when she saw the computer display come to life. She couldn't scramble around the counter fast enough. She nearly knocked Nancy down.

"And you call me clumsy," Nancy remarked, steadying herself.

"Sorry," George apologized. "But this register is way, way cooler than the computer in the window. And it doesn't even have a half-hose driver!" Under the counter, George found the instruction manual and began to read it.

Nancy stepped back to let the experts do their job. "Tell me if you find any clues," she told Bess and George. She pulled out her notebook, flipped it open to the clues page, and waited.

While George read the manual, Bess checked out the mechanical side. She was pressing buttons, switching levers, and flipping dials.

"Everything seems to be just fine," Bess remarked. She was quickly figuring out how the machine worked. After taking some change from her purse, Bess pushed a green button.

The register drawer opened, and Bess put the change inside.

The machine beeped and then reported that there was one dollar and sixty-seven cents in the drawer. Bess took three dimes out of the machine and pressed the green button again. The register recounted the money perfectly to one dollar and thirty-seven cents. "It can even count dollar bills!" Bess said with amazement.

"That's the magic of the computer inside," George reported, looking up from the instruction booklet. "There's a magic eye hooked to a scanner. The scanner is programmed to tell dollar bills from fives and tens and twenties. It can even pick out fifties and one-hundred-dollar bills."

Nancy tapped her pencil on her notebook. The Clue Crew had been checking out the register for ten minutes, and they still didn't have any clues about how the money had disappeared. Nancy was positive that the register held the solution to the mystery. She had really

sharp instincts—that was what made her such a great detective.

"Hey!" Bess suddenly shouted. "I think I found something!" She handed Nancy a small piece of white paper, folded into a little square. "This was in the cash drawer. It was stuck in the bottom of the quarter cup."

"Weird," George said, looking over Bess's shoulder at the white paper. "I guess that because the magic eye only recognizes paper money, it didn't do anything with this blank paper."

"It's not blank," Nancy reported, opening the small square. She held up the paper to show the girls that thirty-five little pencil lines were drawn neatly onto the paper in groups of five.

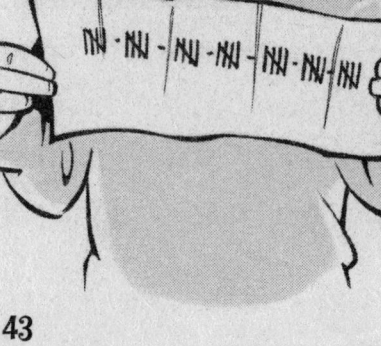

"I wonder what it means," George said softly.

"It's our first clue," Nancy said, writing down *Thirty-five lines* under her clues column.

"I'm not so sure. Maybe it isn't a clue at all." Bess took the paper back from Nancy and refolded it. All the excitement at having found the little piece of paper was gone from her face. "We should probably put it back in the cash register, in case it's something important. Like a code to use if the cash register breaks or something like that."

The girls agreed. Since none of them knew what the paper and the lines meant, they put it back where they found it. But Nancy didn't erase what she'd written about the paper under her clues column.

Nancy knew in her heart that the Clue Crew had just discovered their first clue.

Chapter Six

Gooey, Gooey Clue

"I know where to find a real clue!" Bess said suddenly, moving away from the register. "Come on!" She led the girls to the back of the Pencil Box.

She knocked on Mr. Gustavson's office door, in case he'd come in while they were looking at the register.

"I see you guys knocking," Robin called down from the top of a ladder nearby. "But no one is gonna answer. Mr. G's not here yet." She reached up, pulling a large cardboard box off a high shelf. Then she blew a large pink gum bubble as she balanced the box on one of the ladder rungs.

"Can I help with that?" Nancy asked, stepping toward the bottom of the ladder, prepared to take the box from Robin.

"Huh?" asked Robin, popping the bubble. "Oh." She saw Nancy looking up at her. "I can't hear you." Turning her head, Robin pointed at her ear, reminding Nancy that she still had her music blaring.

"Can I help?" Nancy shouted even louder.

"Nah," Robin replied, finally hearing Nancy's offer. "I'm used to carrying heavy loads. Thanks anyway." Robin put the box on her right shoulder and, using her left hand to steady herself, came down the ladder. "Pencils," she told the girls. "One little box is really light. Put hundreds of little boxes into one bigger box and those pencils are really heavy. I have to get a bunch of these big boxes down today. All the kids are gonna need pencils." She plopped the box of pencils on the floor and turned down her music.

"Do you guys need something in Mr. G's office?" Robin asked.

"I want to see the receipts from yesterday," Bess responded. "I think they might help us sol—"

"I suppose I could let you in," Robin cut in. "Mr. G didn't tell me not to, and seeing as you're working on that upcoming class project and all . . ."

"It's not a class project," George began. "We are investi—"

"Whatever." Robin stopped George's explanation by jingling her shop keys. "Mr. G said I should let you guys look around." She unlocked the door and opened the office. "Have a good time." And with that, Robin blew another big, fat pink bubble and walked away.

"She doesn't listen, does she?" said George as they entered the office.

"Not to us," Bess agreed. "She doesn't let us finish our senten—"

"Whatever," Nancy interrupted, imitating Robin. The girls all laughed. "She's really nice, though."

"And a hard worker," George added. "It's no wonder Mr. Gustavson likes having her work here."

Bess was about to pay Robin another compliment when suddenly she found what she was looking for. She held up the cash register receipt from the previous day. At the bottom, a number was circled in red. "Eight dollars and seventy-five cents," Bess reported.

"Poor Rodger," George moaned, hearing the missing amount of money again. "I hope we can help him."

"We can!" said Bess enthusiastically. "Here's our first clue."

"Our second clue," Nancy corrected.

"All right," Bess gave in. "Since Nancy is such a good detective, we'll go with her instinct. The paper with the thirty-five lines can be our first clue. So this one"—she waved the receipt in her hand—"this is our second clue."

Nancy pulled out her notebook and turned to the correct page, ready for Bess to explain.

"I was thinking about how the cash register weighs the money and can tell how many quarters, dimes, nickels, and pennies are in the drawer," Bess began. "Then I thought, 'I wonder what kind of money was missing?' I mean, was it a five-dollar bill, three ones, and three quarters? Or five one-dollar bills, seventy dimes, and a nickel? It could be almost any combination of money.

"I had to look at the receipt to know for sure." Bess showed Nancy and George the receipt from the cash register. Right above the red-circled "$8.75," it said, "Quarters."

"So," said Nancy with sudden understanding, "the missing money is all in quarters?"

"Exactly." Bess beamed. "Our first"—she looked at Nancy—"I mean, our second clue!"

"Great job," Nancy told Bess as she wrote down the clue in her notebook. "We are cruisin' on the clue finding. Now we need some suspects."

"I have two ideas," George piped up.

Nancy was ready to write.

"Well," George said thoughtfully, "Deirdre had an awful lot of quarters when we saw her at the Drop Zone machine yesterday."

Nancy wrote Deirdre's name under the suspect column. "Good point. That's one. Who's two?"

"Ned Nickerson," George suggested. "He was complaining that the Drop Zone gum loses its flavor, and he needed quarters to get more gum."

"Didn't he say he would get a lot of quarters from his mom?" Bess asked, thinking back.

"No," said George. "He just told us he needed quarters to buy more gum. He never said where he was going to get them." Nancy wrote down Ned's name. Then she studied the names and clues in her notebook. "Deirdre told us that she comes to the mall every day," she said. "I bet if we hang out a while, we can talk to her."

"And how are we going to find Ned?" George wondered.

"He also said he'd be back today to finish his shopping," Nancy recalled. "I can't believe either of them would take money that wasn't theirs, but we'd better check it out."

"Good plan," Bess said. "What about our back-to-school shopping? We promised Hannah we'd get it done today."

"Let's shop now," suggested George. "Schneider's department store is really close. Maybe we can hurry over and get our backpacks, then come back to the Pencil Box before Deirdre and Ned show up."

"Sounds smart to me," Bess agreed.

The girls were leaving Mr. Gustavson's office to go find Hannah when Nancy said, "Ouch." Then someone else yelled, "Auuugghhh." And then there was a crash.

"What happened this time, Nancy Drew?" said Bess, spinning around.

Nancy was holding her toe. "I wasn't looking where I was going and slammed into Robin's ladder."

The girls quickly looked around. Robin's ladder had fallen, and so had Robin. She was lying on the floor under hundreds of Number 2 pencils. In the fall, the big cardboard box she was carrying had opened, and then the little pencil boxes had opened too. There were yellow pencils everywhere.

"Are you okay?" Bess asked, reaching down to pull a pencil out of Robin's spikey hair.

"I'm fine," said Robin, pulling herself up off the ground. She took her earbuds out so she could hear the girls. "How about you?" Robin asked Nancy.

Nancy wiggled her toe to make sure it wasn't broken. "I'm goo—"

"I thought I told you to be careful," Robin interrupted Nancy yet again.

Nancy wondered if Robin might be mad at her, but then the young woman smiled. "Accidents happen," she told them.

"They happen all the time to Nancy Drew," Bess said with a smile. "I mean she's always so—"

"Whatever," Robin cut Bess off. "Hey, help me clean this up, will ya?"

The girls got on their hands and knees to help Robin pick up pencils.

Nancy discovered her purple notebook and matching purple pencil buried under a pile of yellow pencils. She must have dropped them when she bumped her toe.

"Oh, man!" Robin suddenly sat up and grabbed at her throat.

"What?!" The girls popped up and rushed over to Robin's side.

"When I fell off the ladder, I swallowed my gum!" She rolled her tongue around in her mouth, checking that it was gone for sure. "It was a yellow piece," she moaned. "My favorite."

"I thought I saw you chewing pink gum," Bess remarked.

"Pink gum is the worst. It loses flavor in, like, thirty seconds," Robin replied. "Yellow holds it the longest. Maybe five minutes or so." Her shoulders drooped. "Bummer. That piece still had flavor left."

"You didn't swallow your gum," Nancy told Robin with complete certainty.

"I didn't?" Robin asked, confused.

Nancy held up her notebook. There, under the clues column, was Robin's chewed-up yellow gum. It was stuck to the page. "It must have flown out of your mouth when you fell

and then stuck in my notebook," Nancy said, trying to peel the gum off the page without any success.

"Eww," said Bess.

"I don't want my gum back, thanks, but I'm really glad I didn't swallow it," Robin said with a sigh of relief.

"I'm glad you don't want it, because I can't get your gum out of my notebook," said Nancy. "Drop Zone gum might not have good flavor, but it's really sticky."

"It's a bummer that your class project's ruined. Miss Kimler will be so disappointed," Robin said, as she put the last of the pencils in a box. "It's not very nice to turn in your work with gum stuck on it."

"It's not a class pro—" Bess began, then decided to give up. Robin wasn't listening anyway. She'd finished cleaning up the pencils and had stuck her earbuds back in. The music was loud, and Bess knew Robin couldn't hear anything she was saying.

"If she keeps listening to her music that loud, she might go deaf," Bess remarked. "At least, that's what my mom always says." The other girls laughed in agreement.

After Robin went back to work, Bess and George peered into Nancy's notebook.

Bess gave Nancy a little piece of tissue to put over the gum so the notebook pages wouldn't stick together when Nancy closed the purple cover.

"It's official then," George announced. "Robin's gum is our third clue."

Everyone began to giggle.

ChaPTER SEVEN

Quarters, Quarters, and More Quarters

Mr. Gustavson arrived at the store a few minutes before opening time. "Hello, girls," he greeted the Clue Crew. "I see Robin let you in. Any idea where Rodger is?"

Robin pulled the earbuds out of her ears so that she could hear Mr. Gustavson's question. Of course she missed it the first time and had to ask, "What'd ya say, Mr. G?"

"He asked where Rodger was," Bess quickly put in.

"Exactly." Mr. Gustavson nodded. "Where is that boy?" He checked his watch. "On his first day of work, money goes missing from the cash register. On his second day, he's late."

57

Mr. Gustavson tapped his toe on the floor. "Not a good way to impress the boss, if you ask me."

"I'm sure he'll be here in a second," Nancy told Mr. Gustavson. She and the girls had been about to go find Hannah and finally head over to Schneider's to buy those backpacks when Mr. Gustavson arrived at the Pencil Box. Nancy leaned over to Bess and George and whispered, "Hannah and the backpacks are going to have to wait. I think we should hang here and find out why Rodger is late."

The girls agreed to stick around until Rodger showed up. But after five minutes, he still wasn't there. Shoppers were beginning to line up at the counter to pay, and there was no one working the register.

Mr. Gustavson stepped behind the register and began to ring up purchases.

Suddenly Robin came out of the back area, saying, "I know where Rodger is!"

Mr. Gustavson turned to Robin, who was peeling her earbuds out of her ears so that she

could have a conversation and actually hear what was going on, too.

"I nearly forgot!" Robin continued. "I saw Rodger when I came in this morning. He was at the mall early too."

"Where is he, then?" asked Nancy.

"Rodger was waiting for the gaming arcade to open," Robin told everyone around, including the shoppers standing in line. "I asked him what he was doing, and he said he always goes there first thing in the morning. He likes to be the daily high scorer on Thrash Combat." She paused, then added, "Apparently today is a special day. They're having a contest."

Mr. Gustavson stopped ringing purchases long enough to ask Nancy and the Clue Crew kindly, "Would you girls please go over to the arcade and tell Rodger to come to work?" He glanced at the growing line. Back-to-school shoppers were quickly filling the store. "Tell him to hurry. Or he'll be in trouble for more than the missing money."

"Will do, Mr. Gustavson," George said. The girls didn't want Rodger to get into more trouble, so they rushed out of the store to go find him and bring him back. They made a quick stop by Hannah to explain where they were headed. She was busy finishing a sleeve for the sweater she was knitting and was happy to wait for them.

Nancy pulled out her notebook and pencil as they walked through the mall.

She was flipping pages, looking for the Missing Money clues and suspect page and once again not paying attention to where she was going. "Oops. Sorry," Nancy would say as she bumped into shoppers in the crowded mall.

The third time she ran into someone, Bess grabbed Nancy's arm to stop her. "What are you doing?" she asked.

"I'm adding another suspect to our list," Nancy replied, finally finding the right page and lifting her pencil, ready to write.

"Who's the suspect?" George asked. "We

already have Ned and Deirdre. Who else could have taken the quarters?"

Nancy looked across to the arcade. They could see Rodger through the window, standing at a tall video game, pressing buttons wildly. She pointed at the arcade sign.

It read: GAME PLAY PALACE in flashing red neon lights. And under that, in smaller blue letters: ALL VIDEO GAMES 25 CENTS.

The girls looked through the glass at Rodger just in time to see him stop pressing buttons. Then he reached into his jeans pocket, pulled out a coin, inserted it into the game, and resumed playing.

"It must take him a lot of quarters to become the high scorer every day," Bess added, as she realized the connection. "Maybe even eight dollars and seventy-five cents worth of quarters."

"Rodger is definitely a suspect." Nancy wrote down Rodger Hunter's name under the suspect column. "I'm wondering if maybe he needed all those quarters to play Thrash Combat," she explained. "I hate to make him a suspect, but it sure does seem suspicious."

"We have three suspects now," Bess said, as they continued on their mission. There were going not just to get Rodger to come back to the

Pencil Box, but now to also ask him where he got his quarters from.

They'd nearly gone inside the Game Play Palace when someone came up behind the girls and said, "Hey, Nancy. Hi, Bess. Hiya, George." All three girls turned around at the same time to see who was calling their names.

It was Deirdre Shannon. Suspect Number One.

ChaPTER EighT

The One and Only

"Hey, Deirdre," Nancy greeted her. Nancy immediately noticed that Deirdre was holding the same tin that she had been carrying the day before. The lid was on the heart-shaped box today, but Nancy knew what was inside. She'd seen the contents when they'd been standing in line at the Drop Zone. Deirdre's box was full of quarters.

"What's up?" Deirdre asked Nancy, Bess, and George. "You got a new mystery to solve?" Everyone around school knew about Nancy Drew and the Clue Crew.

"We're hot on a case," Bess told Deirdre.

"Tell me more." Deirdre wanted to hear the details.

"Do you know Rodger Hunter?" George asked her. And when Deirdre nodded, she continued, "The cash register he was working on yesterday is missing some quarters."

"Eight dollars and seventy-five cents worth of quarters," Bess said, glancing quickly down at Deirdre's money box.

"Quarters!" Deirdre exclaimed. "I love quarters."

Nancy looked at her note-book. Was it possible that Deirdre had taken the cash register money after all?

"Let me show you mine." Deirdre opened the lid of her tin box and showed Nancy, Bess, and George all her quarters.

Nancy did a quick count and estimated how many quarters were in Deirdre's box. There were probably about forty.

"Wow!" Bess exclaimed. "Why do you have so many?"

"I've been collecting quarters for a few years now." Deirdre ran a finger through her collection. She picked out a quarter to show the girls. "During the summer, I carry them with me everywhere I go just in case I find one I don't already have."

"This is the Ohio quarter. See the airplane and the astronaut?" The girls all bent in to see the small etching on the back of the quarter. "And this," Deirdre said, pulled out another quarter, "is California's. It has a picture of the famous environmentalist John Muir on it." Deirdre was really excited about her collection.

Nancy thought about Deirdre and her quarters. Unless she had a lot of time to go through the cash register and pick out specific coins, there was no way she'd taken any quarters from the register. She was too particular in what she was looking for. But Nancy had to ask two more questions, just to be sure.

"Deirdre, where do you get your quarters?" Nancy asked.

"I go to the bank. I give the teller the dollar bills I earn for my allowance and they give me quarters. It's so easy. The teller will usually go through the drawer and try to find me the states I need. They're really nice like that. Especially Kathy at First Bank here in the mall. She keeps a list of what I need and watches out for them." Deirdre looked at Nancy. "Do you want to start a collection too?"

"No thanks," said Nancy. "But it's fun to look at yours." She had one more question, then she could cross Deirdre off the suspect list. "You said you get gum every day at the Drop Zone. Where do you get those quarters?"

"You sure do have a lot of questions, Nancy Drew. Am I a suspect in your mystery?" Deirdre asked.

"Well, yes," Bess told Deirdre, completely honest.

"Oh," Deirdre said, sort of laughing. "Well

then, you should know that I get my Drop Zone quarters from my dad. Every night he dumps the change out of his pocket onto the top of his dresser. I'm allowed to take the regular, boring, old quarters to put in the gum machine." She opened her mouth to show Nancy, Bess, and George the pink piece she'd already bought that morning. "He hardly ever has any new-looking state quarters," Deirdre said with a sigh.

Deirdre was on her way to meet Kathy at the bank. Kathy had called to say she had a shiny Missouri quarter. "They've been out a while, so shiny ones are hard to find," Deirdre told them.

"Thanks for the answers," Nancy said. "You aren't a suspect anymore."

"No surprise," Deirdre responded. "Good luck with your case. I gotta run. Kathy's waiting for me." She quickly put the lid back on her quarter tin and rushed away.

Nancy made a thick line through Deirdre's name in her notebook.

After reading the list of clues out loud, "Thirty-five lines, quarters, and a wad of ABC gum," Nancy crossed Ned off the suspect list.

"Why are you scratching out Ned's name without even talking to him?" George asked.

"Yeah," agreed Bess. "Until we interview him, he's still a suspect. We don't know where he got all those quarters from yesterday."

"And he kept changing his gum for new pieces," George added. "He said himself that he'd put a lot of quarters in the Drop Zone machine. Maybe he spent a whole eight dollars and seventy-five cents."

Nancy considered her friend's words. "There's no possible way Ned put eight dollars and seventy-five cents into the machine. Ned said that he had ten or eleven pieces and that he ran out of money."

Bess did some quick math. "If he had eight dollars and seventy-five cents to spend," she told the others, "that means that Ned would have chewed thirty-five pieces of gum."

"Whew. That's a crazy lot of chewing," George remarked. "It would take all day to chew that much gum."

Nancy touched her pencil to her notebook. "Ned is off the list. There's only one suspect left."

"Rodger!" Bess and George declared at the exact same time.

"Yep," Nancy confirmed. She was bummed that Rodger was their last and only suspect. "Unfortunately, we've got to tell Mr. Gustavson."

CHAPTER NINE

Bubble Trouble

"Did you find Rodger?" Mr. Gustavson asked Nancy, Bess, and George as they returned to the Pencil Box. He was standing behind the cash register, still ringing up sales. The line had grown since the girls left the store. It wove around the countertop and down Aisle Eight.

"We didn't get him," Bess told the store owner.

"What do you mean?" he asked, wrinkling his eyebrows. "I need him. I can't keep ringing up sales all day. I have office work to do." He pointed at the door to the shop and in a softer, gentler voice continued, "Please, I need you to go get him."

"We need to talk to you first," Nancy said to Mr. Gustavson. "There's something we think you should know."

The girls had decided that they shouldn't tell Rodger to come back to the store. If he did take the money to play video games, Mr. Gustavson wasn't going to want him back anyway. Besides, they knew exactly where he was, and from the way he was stabbing at video game buttons it looked like he'd be there a while. They could always go get him after they told Mr. Gustavson the solution to the mystery.

"Tell me what you discovered," Mr. Gustavson said, taking a credit card from a tall woman in a flowered hat.

"We'd like to tell you in private," Bess told him. "Can we meet in your office, please?"

He surveyed the girls' serious faces and said, "I'll have Robin take over the cash register in five minutes. Go on back to my office. I'll meet you there."

The girls walked down Aisle Twelve to

Mr. Gustavson's office. Robin was standing in the middle of the aisle, putting more tape rolls in the display. She was blowing purple bubble-gum bubbles and listening to her headphones. When she saw Nancy, Robin dramatically threw her body in front of the display. "I've been working on this for an hour," she explained. "Be very careful walking by."

Nancy hugged the opposite side of the aisle and was very careful not to swing her arms. When she reached the end of the aisle, she said suddenly, "I need to see that cash register!" She spun quickly around—and unfortunately, knocked over a display of pens as she turned.

"Augghh!" Robin cried, diving down the aisle in an attempt to stop the pens from spilling everywhere. It was too late. Pens were rolling down Aisle Twelve and into Aisle Fourteen.

Robin told Nancy, "Sit right there and don't move." Then she went off to get a broom and dustpan to help collect the pens.

Robin was only gone a few minutes. Bess and George helped her clean up, but Robin didn't want Nancy to move. She didn't want her to knock over anything else and decided that if Nancy was very, very still, nothing bad could happen.

As she cleaned, Robin blew gum bubbles.

Pop! Pop! Pop! went the green bubbles.

George remarked that Robin had changed from purple to green gum.

"Does green gum hold its flavor?" George asked.

"It's okay," Robin replied. "But yellow is still the best."

Once the mess had been cleaned up and Robin had gone back to work, George asked Nancy, "What was all that excitement about when you knocked over the pens?"

"I don't think Rodger took the money. Really, only one of our clues leads to him, but"— Nancy paused dramatically—"I do think I've solved this mystery. I'll know for sure after I look at the cash register one last time."

"I came as quickly as I could," Mr. Gustavson said, walking toward the girls. "Do you have something to tell me?"

"Nope," Nancy told him, grabbing Bess and George's hands. "We don't have anything to tell you. Not yet, anyway."

Mr. Gustavson looked puzzled. "But you said there was something I should know."

"First we need one last look at the cash register," said Nancy. "Then we'll know for sure what happened to your eight dollars and seventy-five cents."

CHAPTER TEN

Stuck Like Glue

Nancy practically dragged her friends back down Aisle Twelve to the counter where the new cash register sat. A confused Mr. Gustavson followed.

Robin was now at the counter, ringing up sales. She'd taken out her earbuds, but the MP3 player was still hanging around her neck.

"I had a hunch the answer to this mystery was inside that machine," Nancy reminded the Clue Crew. "Now I'm sure it is. Can we open the cash drawer?" she asked Mr. Gustavson.

Robin looked at Mr. Gustavson. "There's a line," she told him. "Can't this wait?"

"We only need a second," Nancy told Mr. Gustavson.

He agreed to give her the time she needed and suggested that Robin take a break. As Robin walked away muttering, "Try not to break the register," she tucked her earbuds into her ears.

"I won't even touch it," Nancy promised, and to prove how trustworthy she was, she stuck her hands deep into her pockets.

Mr. Gustavson apologized to all the people waiting in line and gave them free pencils as a thank-you for being so patient while Bess opened the register and looked inside.

"I want to see that little paper you found before," Nancy told her.

Bess discovered the paper, under a bunch of quarters, still tucked in the bottom of the quarter cup, just like it was the day before. She unfolded it and handed it to George.

"Wait a minute! There are now thirty-eight lines," George reported. "What does it mean?"

Nancy brought her hands out of her pockets and took the piece of paper. "Your mystery is

solved," she told Mr. Gustavson. "Can we tell Robin to come back now?"

Frowning, Mr. Gustavson motioned down the aisle to Robin, who was straightening a stack of computer paper, plugged into her music once more. She hurried back to the register and the waiting line, pulling out her earbuds.

"So what's the solution to the mystery?" Mr. Gustavson wanted to know.

"What mystery?" asked Robin.

"We were working on solving a mystery, not a school project," Nancy explained. "There was money missing from this cash register yesterday."

"I know," Robin said with a shrug. "Eight dollars and seventy-five cents."

"How'd you—" Bess began.

Then Robin, in typical Robin fashion, interrupted, saying, "Because I borrowed it."

"What?" Mr. Gustavson exclaimed. "How? When? Why?"

"Robin took the money to buy gum," Nancy told him. "I have it all figured out—for every

quarter Robin took, she made a little line on this piece of paper." Nancy held up the paper Bess had found in the cash register. "She was planning to pay it back later, right?"

"I do it the same way every day. Always have," Robin said. "Thing is, I was running late

last night to meet my friend at the park, and I didn't get back to the cash register. I figured I'd simply add on today's gum and pay it all back before I went home tonight."

"Oh," said George. "That explains why there are three more little lines on the paper today. We've already seen you chewing purple, green, and now"—she looked in Robin's mouth—"white gum."

"I'm chewing the gum to help stop biting my nails," Robin explained.

"Well, then," Mr. Gustavson said, looking happily around at everyone. "No harm done." He and Robin agreed that she'd repay him all the money she'd spent on gum before the store closed.

"Well, this mystery is in the bag," Nancy told her friends. "We'd better go find Hannah and get cracking on that school supply list."

"What about Rodger?" Bess asked. "Even if he didn't take the money, he's going to be in huge trouble for skipping work to play video games."

"I'm here!" Rodger said breathlessly as he ran into the store. "I'm so sorry I'm late, Mr. Gustavson, but I have amazing news."

"This better be good," Mr. Gustavson told Rodger. He tapped his watch. "You are very, very late for work."

"Yes, but—" Rodger said, trying to catch his breath. It was clear he'd run from the arcade to the shop.

"But what, son?" Mr. Gustavson said patiently.

"I won!" Rodger said. "I won the highest scorer contest on Thrash Combat. The game makers are sending a TV crew over here to interview me." He paused. "And the best part is that the same people who make Thrash Combat invented the Drop Zone. They're sending you a brand-new gumball machine. With more levels and twists and turns and ramps."

"Wow!" Bess clapped her hands. "That is good news."

"There's more!" Rodger exclaimed. "I told

them how the Drop Zone gum loses its flavor, and they promised to send better gum. Gum that stays fresh all day long!"

At that, all the kids in line for the register cheered. But Robin cheered the loudest.

Mr. Gustavson put his arm around Rodger. "Thank you," he said.

"I'm not in trouble anymore?" asked Rodger.

"Not even a little," Mr. Gustavson answered. "But you'd better be at work on time tomorrow." He smiled and Rodger laughed.

"Thank you so much, Clue Crew," Mr. Gustavson said. "I have a present for you, Nancy Drew." Mr. Gustavson gave Nancy a brand-new purple notebook and matching pencil. "Robin told me there was gum stuck to your notebook. This should help you on the Clue Crew's next mystery."

"Thanks, Mr. Gustavson." Nancy couldn't stop looking at the new notebook. The cover had sparkles on it, and the pencil had a fluffy lavender feather instead of an eraser.

Bess, George, and Nancy linked their arms together and walked toward where Hannah was waiting to take them to Schneider's department store. Near the front of the Pencil Box, Nancy accidentally bumped into a display of glue sticks. Luckily, it didn't tip over—just teetered for a second.

"Hannah would have loved it if you'd knocked down that display," said Bess, looking at the glue sticks. "If you'd spilled glue, we really would be stuck together."

"The Clue Crew doesn't need glue to stick together," George replied. "We're already bonded by friendship."

"And a knack for solving mysteries," Bess added.

"Very true," exclaimed Nancy. "The Clue Crew is definitely stuck on mysteries!"

Make Your Own
Back-to-School Notebook!

It's that time of year again! Now that you've been to the mall with Nancy and the Clue Crew, you can make your own bright and flashy back-to-school notebook!

You Will Need:

Spiral-bound notebook

Wide, furry pipe cleaners (of all colors!)

Colored paper

Tacky glue

Glitter

Stickers

A photo of you and your friends

Ready, Set, Note!

❀ First, line up your choice of pipe cleaners in the order you want to stick them on. Then, using the tacky glue, stick the pipe cleaners onto the notebook cover one by one. Let it dry.

❀ Once the glue has dried, fold the ends of the pipe cleaners against the bottom and top edges of the inside cover. To cover up the folded pipe cleaner ends, glue a sheet of colored paper onto the inside cover. This also gives you another surface to decorate!

❀ Once the inside cover dries, glue on the photo of you and your friends, and decorate it with your favorite stickers!

❀ For more sparkles, dot the front cover with glue and sprinkle on some glitter!

❀ Get creative! Try using beads, buttons, feathers, or ribbon to give your notebook more flair!

Remember Fun and Fuzzy Days!

❀ To make your back-to-school notebook extra special, decorate the back of your notebook too! Then leave room for an end-of-year photo with your friends. That way when school finishes, you'll be able to see how much you all have changed!

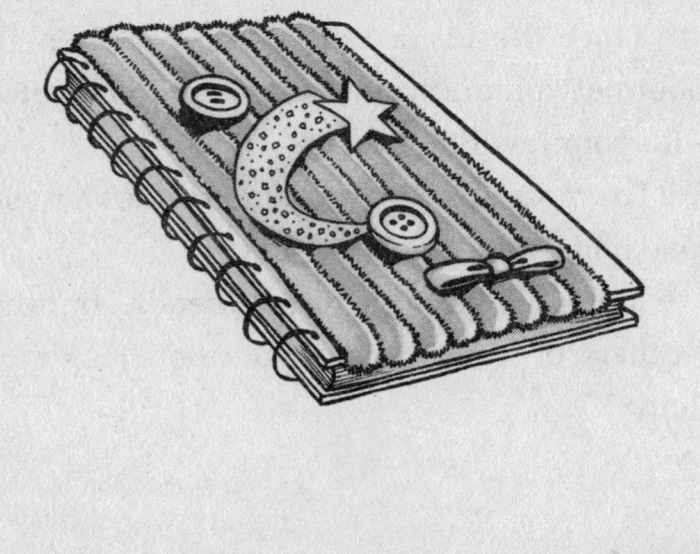